# After the Storm
## Book 3 "New York"
### By Don Chase

**For my Mom.**
**I still miss you every day.**

Chapter 1


**"I'M NOT GETTING A PULSE!"** Chris was screaming. I could barely hear her at all and she was right next to me.

**"CHECK AGAIN!"** I yelled as more shells landed scant yards away from us.

"I've checked five times honey, he's gone," she said sadly as she stood up.

**"GEORGE IS NOT FUCKING DEAD! GET HIM OVER TO THE DOCS AND KEEP FUCKING CHECKING UNTIL YOU FIND SOMETHING,"** I bellowed at the love of my life. Right at this moment though, I couldn't bear to look at her.

"But Mack…" she started to say, before I cut her off. "Just do as your fucking told!" I snapped as I heard more bombs go off around us.

"I will, but I don't think it will help," she said before she sighed and turned to find someone to help her with the body.

"Thank you," I muttered as I waited until the next set of shells fell before running out of the ruined restaurant. I jogged across the tiny road to what used to be a post office. It was a good solid concrete and brick building with a very deep basement. It was the one place in the last few days that I felt even slightly safe.

The soldier at the door gave me a curt nod as I came in. Returning it, I walked quickly across the once shiny floor to the granite steps that would lead me downstairs. There was another guard outside an old wooden door. He too gave a nod as I pushed my way in, letting it fall shut on its own behind me.

"Hello Duncan," Brett Twombly said.

"Hey," I said, looking around our war room. Brett was standing at the far end of the long folding table with Art, Mike, Hags and a couple other clan chiefs as well as Roy and Teddy.

"You're late," Roy chided jokingly.

"Sorry, something came up," I said simply.

"Ah the troubles of command," Brett said nodding knowingly.

"I suppose you can be forgiven, at least you beat George here," Teddy said chuckling.

"George won't be here," I said moving to the far end of the room.

"Tied up?" Brett asked, sounding perturbed.

"George has been hurt. He's being taken back further behind the lines, so they can fix him up," I said calmly.

"What happened?"

"Is he okay?"

"How badly is he hurt?"

The questions kept coming. Everyone wanted to know what happened. **"SHUT UP!"** I yelled, punching the table, "I dunno what happened okay? One second, he was behind me, the next thing I know a round went off outside and people started screaming. I looked around and he was on the floor. That's all I know, I swear, so can we just move on?" I asked, dumping myself heavily into an old wooden chair at the table.

Roy slid me a tumbler filled with something resembling whiskey. I picked it up and drained it before giving him a nod.

"Of course, I'm sure he'll be fine. Where were we?" Brett asked.

"We were just reviewing how badly we were getting crucified out there. I swear the shelling hasn't stopped for three days, at least," Hags said scratching at his heavy scruff.

"You'd think they'd run out of them at some point," Teddy said, shrugging.

Their voices started to fade out as I stared blankly at the group of men that were working, feverishly to keep us all alive. Hags was right, it had been three days. I had been awake for all of it. The beating we had taken that pushed us back here was brutal, and then the shelling started. I was running on fumes and had no idea how much further I could push.

Teddy laughed about something, and it sounded like it was coming down a hollow pipe a mile away. I reflexively turned toward him and saw how ragged he looked, while wondering how much worse I must seem. We didn't always look this way. At least, not back in Boston and that was only a couple months ago…

The battle of the Mass. Ave. Bridge had been about three months back. After we had run the troops out of Boston, I had initially tried to just hide in my little section of the world. Within a month, Brett, Hags, and Matt had done their damndest to change that. If they weren't sending runners to ask for something, they were showing up themselves.

Eventually, it worked and our clan started integrating themselves into Brett's idea of some odd little collective. After we started working closer together, he informed me that he had been sending runners both north and south of us, to get a feel for what was going on in the surrounding states. He had discovered that there were whole sections of the northeast that had no troops in them, with decent sized clans, just waiting for someone to contact them. Within a short period of time, we began seeing clans from as far north as Bangor, Maine, trickling into our area and setting up shop. Thankfully, most of them brought their own food and equipment. One thing I can say for northerners is that they travel prepared.

Our numbers had swollen significantly. Before they had even finished setting up their camps, Art and George had come up with a plan to take out the small contingents of troops stationed in Portsmouth, New Hampshire and Portland, Maine. The way George figured it, that would free up the whole northeastern coastline from Canada to the northern border of Connecticut. Not a small feat for a bunch of untrained morons.

We had heard back from the southern states. What was left of Rhode Island was pretty willing to join our cause, as well as Connecticut. They unfortunately, had a battalion of troops stationed throughout the area, making moving large groups of people and equipment difficult. They were more than happy to join us, but they needed help getting rid of the troops. That made Connecticut our first stop when we started our trip.

In the mean time, Brett and the other clan chiefs had formed a loose infrastructure that looked, a bit too much, like a formal government in my opinion. They did this in anticipation of our new arrivals from the other states. They wanted to show a united front in the face of an overpowering aggressor, or some such nonsense. I was again approached to be in charge of our military forces and once again I refused. Actually, I refused several times. I eventually caved in and acquiesced, allowing them to anoint me as commanding general of the united clans.

Drake, George, and just about everyone else, had a grand old time referring to me as mon generale, generalisimo, my personal favorite Admiral Akbar, and any other number of supposedly witty comments.

"What do you think general?" I heard someone asking.

"Hmm?" I said snapping out of my reverie.

"I was just saying that it might be a good idea to send men out to find us a new location. Something a bit further away, in case they decide to push us again?" Brett asked eyeing me curiously.

"Yeah, that sounds like a good idea. We wanna know where to go. I'm hoping we won't have to," I said running my hand through my filthy hair.

After getting my approval, they went back to planning our fallback position. They quietly discussed areas on the large map, which might have suitable buildings and access roads. I half listened for a few minutes before I got up from the table and walked to the front of the room to refill my tumbler. I swirled the whiskey in the bottom of my glass, thinking about George, wondering if he was okay, or even still alive. I could hear him in my head laughing at me.

"Y'know, they'd let up on the jokes if you just accepted that you were in charge of more than just our little group," he said smiling.

"I know; I just hate the whole stupid thing. Hell, I don't even agree with uniting the clans. Why the fuck do I want to put up with all of their problems as well as all of ours?" I asked as I paced the comm. center in the shop.

We had moved back in a couple weeks after getting rid of the troops. I figured they wouldn't be coming back anytime soon. We had much better access to the rest of the town from the shop as opposed to the hospital up on the hill. George had set up an antenna there though, which boosted our radio range from the shop significantly. We still had to use relays to get a hold of Hags in town, but we could at least talk to a couple of the towns directly adjacent to us.

"There is always the theory of safety in numbers," George said with a smarmy look on his face.

"Safety from what? If I remember correctly, we just got rid of any immediate threat for the foreseeable future," I said leaning against his desk.

He just laughed at me and shook his head, "You can fight it all you want, but you're only causing yourself more agony. It wouldn't hurt nearly as much, if you just went with it."

"When have I ever done that?" I asked.

"True," was all he said, "You might wanna try it some time."

He was right; in the end, it was easier for me to just accept the role and responsibilities. I got to name my staff and assistants, which were of course Drake, George, Teddy, Tom, and Gomez. I figured if I had to suffer, then so did they. Everyone got assigned a rank and a job, as well as preferential treatment when we had to go visit other clans. In the beginning, it was pretty cool and easy. There wasn't much required at first. Mostly, it was just the occasional meeting or answering a runner. It wasn't until much later, that being the commanding general of the united clans became one of the suckiest jobs I'd ever had.

## Chapter 2

"You seem distracted," Hags said, as I came back from staring into the bottom of my glass.

"Yeah, and tired," I answered.

"Worrying about George?" he asked.

"Mostly, Drake too," I said, glancing around to see that the room was now almost empty.

"When's he due back?" Hags asked, leaning against the table.

"Not until tonight at least, he and the rest of Alpha went to probe the edges of their lines, to see if there were any holes we could exploit. It wouldn't be so annoying, if I could be out there too, or at least be within radio range," I sighed and drained my drink.

"You know that you're needed here more. We really can't afford to have you getting killed. Troop morale would go straight to shit," he said with a shrug.

"Knowing it doesn't make me feel any better about it. It's still annoying," I grumbled.

"I'm sure he and Alpha are fine. They're some of the best men we have," he said.

"You're right, I just have always hated not knowing." I gave a small smile.

"They'll be back soon," he said, clapping me on the shoulder as he stood. "I'll be back in a bit. I gotta go check on my brother and Steve. They were trying to get some generators we found up and running."

"Power would be helpful," I nodded as I grabbed a seat. Teddy and Roy were still here with me and waited for Hags to be well gone before they started in.

"Okay, so now are you going to tell us what's really going on?" Roy asked, knowing I wasn't being fully up front.

I spent the next few minutes going over what had happened to George and how **MOST** of what I had said had been true. I then proceeded to fill them in on how Chris couldn't find a pulse, and how I had her take him further back behind to find one. Roy just nodded, listening. Teddy had been listening too and was visibly shaken by the fact that one of our closest friends may, or may not be dead. He shoved his chair back and stood quickly, heading for the door.

"Hold up," I said, cutting him off at the end of the long table.

"I'm gonna go check on him," he said trying to sidestep me.

"Just wait a sec Teddy," I said, stepping in front of him. "We have to be prepared for the fact that he may already be gone."

He stared silently at me for a moment, then tilted his head at me slightly, "Well, if you fucking cared enough to be back there with him, then I'm betting we'd already know how he was, wouldn't we?" Teddy asked as he straight armed me, pushing me to the side.

"Excuse me?" I said, feeling as if someone had just punched me in the face.

"You fuckin' heard me. Unlike you, I'm not gonna stay up here being cool, while my best friend bleeds out on me alone," he said, pulling open the door while glaring at me.

"What the fuck?" I said as I jammed my mud covered boot up against the heavy wooden door, keeping it from opening wider. "Seriously, what the fuck did you just say to me?" I asked as I grabbed Teddy by the collar of his shirt and shoved him hard up against the cold concrete wall.

"This wouldn't have happened if we had fucking minded our own business and stayed in Boston!" he spat at me.

**"ENOUGH!"** Roy yelled as he shoved me off of Teddy. "Cut the shit, if you idiots would stop for a second, you'd realize that you're both doing this because none of us have slept for days."

We looked at each other and then hung our heads. Teddy mumbled something about being sorry, and I gave him a nod. I leaned against the wall and sighed as I squeezed my eyes shut tight, trying and get the burning to go away, it didn't work.

"I'm gonna go check on George, I can send back word if you'd like," Teddy said, holding the door open waiting for me to answer.

"Yeah, that'd be great actually, seems I'm pretty worried about him, even if I don't want to admit it," I said with a small smile.

"'Course you are, he's family," Teddy said as he smiled and left.

"We're just all real tired Mack, don't be too mad at him," Roy said as he gave my shoulder a squeeze.

"Nah, I'm not mad, you're right we're all just beat to shit. Try and go get some rest buddy. That is, if you can sleep through this shelling," I said as we both left the war room and headed up the concrete steps.

"A, it has to stop sometime, and B, with enough booze, I can sleep anywhere," Roy said as he pushed open the post office door.

"I'm gonna stay here and check the comm. center to see if Drake has checked in. I'll talk to you a bit later," I said, giving him a wave.

"I'm gonna try and find a quiet spot in a basement to grab some sleep," he said with a grin as he trotted off down the road away from the incoming shells.

We were holed up in a town just outside of New York City called Larchmont. It looked like every other small town we had passed through, or camped in on our way down here. We had just about made it into the city itself, when we came across a large force that had artillery support. After taking a merciless beating, we had to pull back and rethink our head on strategy.

We had about two thousand men total. That many men and equipment is not easy, or fast to move long distances. I often found myself wishing to be back at home. It was much easier to only have to worry about the ten to twenty guys that we used to take on our missions. Hell, it takes two hours just to pack up our camp and get ready to move every day. It seemed to take us forever to get into Connecticut, much less through it.

I looked out the door, at what used to be a productive small town. From what we could tell, it was deserted now and had been for a while. It was a bunch of empty buildings that had been picked clean before whoever was left, up and moved on. It was by no means an ideal location, but we needed a place to regroup and this section of town had brick and concrete storefronts instead of wooden houses. We figured the buildings could withstand the shelling better. We set up most of our command stuff in the post office. The rest of the buildings in the area were to store men and equipment. The restaurant across the street was mainly a small triage area where Chris was assessing people's injuries. Most were patched up right there, but the more severe wounds were sent back to a clinic we had set up further down the road where they would be safer.

I walked up a short set of steps and across the main lobby. We had a makeshift radio set-up that Gomez had put together on a long wooden counter. I talked to the guy on duty, and asked if Drake, or any of the others from Alpha, had checked in. After a moment, he told me that they had not. I thanked him and gave him a smile, that I'm sure must have looked fake. Drake had only been gone a few hours. I hated the fact that I wasn't out there with them. The plan had been that they would stay on route 1 as long as possible and get as close as they could to the city to see if they could find a hole in the army's defenses. He promised me they'd be back by dark, so that gave him another couple of hours before I could really start to worry.

I walked across the small street to the triage center, hoping that Chris was back with news about George. I found instead, a very pregnant Sam, who hadn't seen Chris since she left. She was busy helping, as best she could, with making the wounded as comfortable while they waited for one of the doctors to get to them. We hadn't lost as many men as I had feared when we started getting our asses handed to us three days ago. The amount of wounded had been a bit of a surprise.

It had been a running battle for almost two days. Today had really been the first time to settle in and take an accurate count of the dead and wounded. The triage unit was starting to get back under control. Late last night, when we first established a perimeter here, it was horrifying. I still don't know how Chris and her people do this without wanting to kill themselves.

I hadn't wanted to bring Chris with us, mostly for my own peace of mind. I remember distinctly that fight not lasting very long. Hell, she even threatened to go over my head and bring her protest to Brett. She kept pointing out to me that she and her team were the best suited to deal with any of the battle injuries we may incur. She then drove home the point repeatedly, by reminding me that stitching up me and my teams for years is what prepared them for this. I love my dear wife very much. She used to be very mild and soft spoken. Sometimes, I think we may have created a monster, a cute monster, but a monster no less.

I stayed with Sam for a bit, changing dressings and trying to help as much as possible. I wasn't very good at this end of things, but I did what I could. I was hoping that Chris would get back while I was here, but after an hour and a half she was still, nowhere to be found. Sam saw that the sun was starting to go down and asked me about Drake. I gave her a quick kiss on the head and told her that I'd go check to see if they were back. She gave me a small smile as I walked out. She hated him being out there as much as I did, but for different reasons. He was about to be a dad for the first time and really disliked the idea of him getting killed.

As I started to walk across the street I stopped. It was quiet, really quiet. It hadn't struck me before, but there was no shelling, hadn't been for about a half hour, now that I thought back. I suddenly felt an almost panic as I bolted up the stairs to the post office. Busting through the doors, I saw the kid on the radio was stressed. He was pale and sweating as he listened hard to the headphones he was wearing. The other people in the room were buzzing with activity.

"What the hell is going on?" I barked as I made my way over to the radio operator.

"This just started coming in. You should probably hear it" he said handing me the headphones.

"Should I go get the rest?" someone asked him.

"No need, the general is here now, but thanks," he answered as I slid the headphones on.

"I repeat, Papa Bear this is Alpha one we are two miles out and coming in hot," I heard Drake, saying over and over. I pulled off the headset and tossed it back to the radio guy.

"Tell him to keep coming hard and that he should have help a mile out," I said as I ran for the front door.

"Yes sir," he said.

I grabbed the guard at the door, telling him to run over to the makeshift barracks we had set up on the corner of the street and get me ten men. As he took off, I trotted over to the triage building and picked up my AK that I had left there earlier. I came out and saw Gomez who had heard what was going on from his radio man. He was geared up and ready to go. We jogged down to the end of the street and hooked a right onto the main stretch that ran out of town. By the time we had gotten to the end of the block the door guard and at least a dozen men were behind us, all running to catch up. Gomez tapped me on the shoulder and pointed to his ear. I instantly understood and fumbled around in my shirt pocket for my ear bud. Obviously, someone wanted to get a hold of me.

"Mack here," I said.

"Where exactly do you think you're going?" I heard Brett say.

"I'm going out to make sure my best friend gets back here alive. Shouldn't take too long," I said.

"We have people that are better suited to get that done general," he sounded pissy as he stressed the rank.

"I'm sure we do, look I'll be fine..." I started to say.

13

"That's not the point," he said, cutting me off. "You can't go running off every time you feel like it,"

"Okay Brett, we'll do it this way then. This is a military operation and I am in control of the military. That means I get to tell you to shut the fuck up and leave me alone. In case you didn't notice, I'm a little busy. In the mean time, tell the radio guy to tell Alpha to switch over to the ear buds. We should be close enough. Thanks, bye now," I said with a smirk. I'm not entirely sure, but I think I may have heard Brett swear as he got off the line.

After a minute, I heard another voice in my ear, "Alpha one here."

"Where you at?" I asked.

"Hey Mack, we're coming through the woods off the side of the road. It was getting too hot out in the open," Drake said.

"Okay, we're on our way into the woods now. Don't shoot anything in front of you," I said pointing toward the tree line fifty yards off to my left.

"Copy that. Be advised, we have at least a dozen on our tail," he said, sounding out of breath.

"Copy, no problem, I'm bringing friends," I replied.

We plowed headlong into the woods, spreading out to have a wider field of fire to help cover Alpha. Within a couple minutes you could hear the crack of rifle shots and the trampling of dead leaves as Alpha got closer. I still couldn't see any of them, but it made me move a bit faster in the direction of the noise. I heard the rattle of an M-16 and caught movement off to my right, just before I saw Tom come crashing through a bush and fall on his face, a couple rounds buried themselves in the tree next to him.

"Tom!" I exclaimed.

"Mack, sweet Jesus!" he said as he scrambled behind the tree and dropped the mag out of his rifle.

"You on point?" I asked as I took cover behind the tree next to him, scanning out in front of me, trying to find the rest of the team.

"Yeah, Drake's covering our asses, he told us to run. I have no idea how far back he is," he said, trying to catch his breath.

"Everyone stay sharp, I found the point man, Alpha should be close by," I said so the rest of my men knew there were friendlies nearby.

"Here they come!" I heard Gomez yell off to my left. I caught a glimpse of another three members of Alpha as they darted in and out of the dead trees.

We kept moving forward as they bolted through our lines. One of them threw himself down on the ground behind a bush while another ducked behind a tree with his hands on his knees desperately trying to catch his breath. "They're close. Couldn't see Drake," he said, gasping.

I picked up speed and started jogging in the direction they had just come from. That quickly changed to running, as I heard more than a couple M-16's open up. I finally saw the first group of troops and fired off a burst. Gomez and some of the others did the same. I heard rustling coming toward me and swung my AK to meet it. Drake came bursting out between a small group of trees just as rounds snapped over our heads and hit the trees around us.

He barreled into me and we both almost went down. Looking at me wide eyed, and holding my shoulder to keep himself upright he yelled, **"RUN, I MISCOUNTED!"**

I looked up, into the dead forest around me, and saw how right he was. There was a line of troops, less than fifty yards behind him. There had to be at least twenty five to thirty five, all strung out sweeping through the woods, firing at anything that moved. "Fall back, fall back now!" I hissed into the mic, grabbing a hold of Drake and shoving him in front of me as we both moved back toward town.

"Holy shit!" I heard Gomez say in my ear just before a loud burst from multiple rifles erupted behind us, **"MOVEMOVEMOVE!"** he yelled in one long word.

Some of the men that had been further back tried laying down cover fire as we retreated. After we got behind them and near the tree line, we turned to return the favor. The troops had closed the gap between us. We managed to take down a half a dozen, or so. Once everyone caught up, we spread out and tried to find some cover.

"We can't stay here," Gomez said as he peeked out from behind his tree about ten feet to my left.

"We're almost at the tree line. Once we get out in the open we're even more fucked," Drake said.

"Nah, you'll be fine ya big puss," I heard Roy say in my ear.

"Huh?" I said.

"Seriously, just bolt for the tree line guys, it's all good I promise," Roy said.

"You heard the man, lay down some rounds and let's move," Gomez said as he stood and opened up blindly, deeper into the forest.

The dozen, or so, men and the rest of Alpha joined him. They then, turned and quickly made their way the last ten yards or so, out of the forest and into the open field near town. Drake and I were still inside, watching to make sure the troops were still following. They had taken cover, but were now back up and closer than I would have liked. We fired short bursts and moved back a bit, covering each other as we went.

"You ready old man?" Drake asked with a grin.

"As I'm gonna be," I replied. We both stood and emptied our clips before turning, and bolting out into the field. Rounds snapped over our heads as I saw what Roy was talking about. He had come into the field with a couple of the trucks that we had taken from the Boston troops. To be exact they were the Humvees with the .50 caliber machineguns mounted on top. I watched as Gomez and the men got safely to the Humvees. They quickly turned and took cover behind them, to be able to return fire. We were just about halfway to the makeshift skirmish line when I heard Roy in my ear again, "Down," was all he said.

Drake and I dove head first, into the hard packed ground, covering our heads as a roar of gunfire erupted. Damn the .50's were loud. I peeked behind me; careful to not raise my head too high and saw the first three feet of the tree line behind me disappear under the barrage of gunfire. I'm guessing that Roy had waited until he had seen the troops clear enough, but I honestly, am not sure. After almost a minute, the gunfire tapered off. I heard Gomez give the "All clear," before rolling over and sitting up to look toward the forest. I waited a good long time with no movement or incoming fire, before I stood up. Gomez sent a squad in to check for bodies, take care of wounded and gather weapons, while I walked over to Roy standing happily behind his still smoking .50.

"Hey boss," he said with a smile.

"Thanks for the save," I said, grinning.

"Anytime sir," he said.

"How'd you know where we were?" Gomez asked as he approached.

"Brett told me, he came and found me. Boy, is he pissed," Roy said.

"Oh, I'm sure he is," I said with a shrug. "I'll deal with that in a little bit."

"Yeah, let's get home and get Alpha debriefed first. I may have found our way in," Drake said, grinning.

"Outstanding!" Roy said, "Get in, I'll give you guys a ride."

## Chapter 3

"I believe we've talked about this Duncan," Brett said to me with his hands on his hips.

"I believe I don't give a good fuck," I replied, spinning my glass tumbler on the long wooden table in the basement of the post office.

"As a leader in this government, it is unacceptable to take the risks and put yourself in the danger that you did earlier today. Our people need you to lead, not fight their battles anymore," he said as if he were speaking to a small child.

"As a leader in this government and the head of its' military operations, I have the authority and autonomy of running MY operations any way I see fit. If you remember correctly, I didn't actually want this job to begin with," I said, pushing my chair from the table and standing up, "I've given command of my team to Drake and stayed back behind the front lines of every battle we've had to date. In my opinion, I've given up more than enough."

"I understand that Duncan, but you have to see that we need you..."

"Alive, yeah I get it. You may not understand this, or even like it, but this is how I lead my men. I don't tell them to run out and die if I'm not running out there with them. I've given you all the concessions I can give you. I'm not going to sit by and watch my friends and family die in the field if I can save them. It just isn't going to happen, not now, not ever. I'm sorry if you can't accept that, but you wanted me in this little fucked up idea of a government, and now you're just gonna have to live with it," I said as I clapped him on the shoulder. "Oh yeah, don't ever openly dissent against my decisions again by the way, it looks bad to the men."

I left the room in the basement and walked up the stairs. We had had this same argument months ago back in Boston, more than once. The high council, as I called them, which was made up of Brett Twombly, Hags and Matt Wise hated the idea of me leading by example. I, on the other hand, hated being left behind and not able to watch over my men.

One of the biggest arguments happened at the shop one afternoon. I was just about to go to Burlington to have a little chat with Joe Brunner and his clan up on the hill in the old movie theater. We had argued for almost an hour about them wanting me to send someone else. I stormed out of that one as well. Thankfully, Drake was waiting in the car with Teddy all ready to go. George told me later, that it took him almost two hours and a good bottle of scotch to calm them down after I left.

Drake had rebuilt the interceptor in the weeks after the troops were sent packing and we had a nice leisurely drive over to Burlington. It was as leisurely as a drive through hostile territory can be anyway. He had replaced the axel and fixed the engine. As well as made a few modifications, so that it was more fuel efficient and replaced the back window with a piece of bullet proof glass he had found somewhere. It wasn't the prettiest car I had ever been in, but it did make us feel safer.

We were going to Burlington to talk to Joe Brunner to see if he was going to become part of our little party. At the moment, we were the only game in town that could give him and his people any kind of significant aid. He had been dealing with the military. Now that they were gone, we needed to know if he was with us, or if he was someone we needed to watch. For the most part, what we were going to do wasn't all that dangerous. We were just going to talk. Granted, we were going to talk about him being a lying, backstabbing, traitor, so I guess it could get a bit dangerous.

We had sent a runner a couple days earlier letting him know that we were coming. We didn't tell him specifically, what we were coming for, but he did at least know we were coming. We drove up the steep hill leading to the multi-plex and parked much closer to the doors than we had the last time we had come here.

"Man, I can see why they have the snowmobiles," Drake said as he threw the interceptor in park.

"No shit huh?" Teddy said. "It was ten times worse the last time."

It was spring now, which meant it was slightly warmer and there were a couple less inches of snow. The only time it got warm now days was the middle of summer, even then it wasn't that warm. The days of hitting one hundred degrees in August were long gone.

As we got out of the car, I noticed one of the door guards was the same from the last time I was here. I gave him a nod that he returned as the three of us walked up the stone stairs. I was waiting for them to tell us that we needed to leave our rifles outside, but they never did. I'm guessing that had something to do with the friendliness of our last visit and the fact that we knew Eva, who just happens to be Joe's step sister.

"Hey sexy," she said as she gave me a big hug and a quick kiss.

"You were waiting for us? How sweet," I said, returning the warm hug.

"Of course I was, isn't like we get many visitors, especially old friends," she said as she gave Teddy the same reception. "Well, mostly old friends," she said as her demeanor changed completely while she eyed Drake.

"Seriously, the end of the world came and went and I STILL can't be forgiven for something that happened over a decade ago?" he asked.

"I suppose you can," she said as she leaned in and gave him a quick hug. "You're still an asshole though."

"Good enough for me," he said with a smile.

"Isn't like she's wrong," Teddy said, snickering.

"C'mon boys, Joe's in his office," she said, motioning us to follow her. Her brown hair was tied back loosely in a ponytail and bounced as she led us down back. I glanced over my shoulder catching both Teddy and Drake watching her walk in front of us. I just smiled and shook my head. She was a beautiful girl of just about five feet tall with lightly freckled cheeks and gorgeous bright green eyes. I noticed that her jeans were a tad tighter than they were the last time we were here. I wondered to myself if she was hoping for Drake to show up, or if it was just coincidence.

She gave a quick knock on the office door and I heard Joe inside tell her it was open. She smiled and stepped aside so we could get by her. "Don't you leave without saying goodbye," she said as I went through the door.

"Wouldn't dream of it hon," Teddy said with a wink.

The office was bright compared to the rest of the building. It was one of the few places in the complex that had electric light in it. Joe sat behind his desk; he looked up from whatever he was doing and waved us over. "Have a seat gentlemen. I've been expecting you," he said, reaching into a drawer and pulling out a mostly full bottle of Jack.

The rest of the conversation kind of went downhill from there. We explained to Joe how we knew that he had a deal going on with the military. He, of course, denied it. Then we went round and round from there for a bit. At some point, Eva came in because of the raised voices, which made him try and save face even more. In the end, he lost a lot more than his pride.

After hearing what her step brother had done, she decided that it was time for her and her sister to move on. She was angry because she was sure that she could no longer trust Joe. She stormed out of the room. I dismissed her threats to leave as just that. I continued on, telling Joe about our newly budding organization of clans. To his credit, he listened even being as upset as he was. I let him know that if he still wanted to receive aid of any kind, whether it be medicine or food, he should strongly reconsider his loyalties, because the military wasn't coming back into town anytime soon. He thanked me through gritted teeth and assured me that he would be in touch with us soon. He quickly showed us how to get out of his office.

It was not, to his dismay, quick enough though. Eva was waiting in the lobby with her sister and two medium sized, beat up, old gym bags. I watched as they quietly argued about ten feet away from us, it quickly got louder. Within a minute, it went from loud to dangerous. Joe grabbed Eva by the arm. We being a bit overprotective, of the once young girl we remembered, all drew our weapons. All three were trained directly on Joe. Joe's men decided that they didn't want to be left out and drew their weapons as well, pointing them at us.

Cooler heads prevailed, kind of. We grabbed Eva and her sister. Then we had a lovely little standoff all the way out the door. It wasn't until we were in the car and driving down the hill, that I even remember breathing. We were hoping that given a few days, Joe may send a runner. It took a week, but finally, he did. He once again told us of his allegiance to the cause and that he would gladly help in any way possible. He also wanted to tell his sister that he was sorry. Her response to her brothers' plea was a big "Fuck you!" She seemed pleased with her new home and they both settled in quickly. Anne had remembered her from when she was very young and the two got along quite well almost instantly. Chris was always happy to have another girl around. The only one who seemed unhappy about the whole thing was Drake, Teddy was ecstatic.

By the time I got over to the barracks where Drake and the rest of Alpha was staying, I had a small smile on my face. Drake had been distraught for the first couple of weeks having Eva around to torment him. The boys had cleaned up and were relaxing a bit in one of the common rooms on the second floor. I watched from the doorway, for a moment, as Drake pointed out locations on the folding map of the area.

It was interesting watching him lead Alpha by himself now. We had done it together for years, so I in no way doubted his capabilities to do the job well. It was just an odd and unwelcome feeling being on the outside. I was no longer in charge, or even a part of Alpha. It had changed a bit in the last few months, but it still felt like it should be our team. We had lost AJ and Tim who had been members from the start of all of this, as well as my spot being vacant. It seemed to take us forever to fill the three slots, but we finally did.

Eric Kotter was the first replacement we assigned. He was a good man that we had known for years before the storm. Eric stood about 5'8. I know this because I'm the same height, he was in his late thirties, had long brown hair, with a bit of grey showing through, and eyes that weren't quite sane all the time. After the storm he had become a bit of a recluse that lived on top of one of the many hills in Menotomy. He found a deserted cul-de-sac and moved himself in to the last house on the street. He really enjoyed the idea of being as far removed from people as possible, while still remaining in town.

He showed up at the shop shortly after the Battle of the Mass Ave. Bridge to tell us he was bored. We put him to work helping us rebuild the shop and discovered that he was whiz at small arms and liked to play with explosives. From what I could remember, he had worked at a battery company before the world went to shit and liked to make things go boom, which I hadn't known. After a couple weeks of him being around, we asked if he wanted to join Alpha. He hesitated for a bit, but soon accepted. "If I'm not around some day, it means I decided I wasn't having fun anymore," was how he laid out his terms of service to us.

Woodsie was sitting next to him on a beat up old couch listening to Drake. Bill Woods had come down from somewhere up north. He was a huge man. He stood at about 6'3 and had shoulders that were so wide they barely fit through doors. Both Teddy and Gomez had taken a shine to him instantly. It helped that Woodsie, as he told us to call him, was an incredibly nice guy who was always smiling and joking. One day when we were working at putting the shop back together, Gomez mentioned that we should consider putting Woodsie in with Alpha. I considered it and soon asked the gentle giant if he'd like to join us.

He enthusiastically agreed and began training with Gomez and Drake almost daily. He had known how to use guns long before we had come along, but we were training him to carry our M-60. Not the hardest weapon in the world, but we still wanted to make sure he could handle it. A few days into his training, we agreed that he'd be fine and he'd been a part ever since.

Taking the third open spot in Alpha was Jim. Jim had lived over in Somerville. When the clans started growing closer and uniting a bit more he volunteered to join the military side of things. This led him to spending a good amount of time at the shop. He eventually, moved his family to an empty house, just outside the center of Menotomy, so he'd be closer to where he was working. Jim was about 5'10 and had close cropped brown hair and a very square jaw. He had military training and had served in some hot spots over a decade earlier. He was out of the Army, where he had served as a ranger, by the time the storm hit, but he had kept himself in decent shape. He seemed to fit right in with the other members of Alpha and it was nice having the team back up to strength.

Drake noticed me leaning in the doorway. He stopped talking and motioned me in. "I was just going over the details while we waited for you," he said.

"I was just taking in the view from the outside for a change," I said.

"You're always gonna be one of us," Tom said smiling.

"We couldn't get rid of you if we tried… and we have," Drake said with a smirk.

We talked for over an hour as Drake ran me through the details of his mission and his plan to get us into New York City itself. He answered just about every question I could think of and had his bases pretty well covered. It wasn't perfect, by any means, but it was the best idea we had at the moment. I told him that we could take it to the others tomorrow. He agreed and we spent the rest of the evening going over the details again and again.

The shelling started again around midnight, making sleep difficult, if not impossible. I had grabbed a room in the barracks and dozed off for a bit it seemed. The first round had to have landed a hundred yards away. It was still loud enough to get me to bolt upright. They didn't seem to be aiming at anything in particular, but they were coming close enough to worry me. Drake poked his head into my room shortly after they started. His hair was down and he had a shirt tossed over his shoulder. "Is this more harassment ya'think?" he asked, buttoning his shirt.

"Not sure, they had stopped for a few hours there. They may be coming to get their guys that never came home," I said tying my boots.

"Yeah, I thought of that too. The rest of Alpha is grabbin' their shit. We'll be ready to roll in a sec," he said before he turned to go gather his men.

I sighed and rubbed my eyes. Standing, I stretched and heard everything crack and pop. I grabbed my AK and headed out into the hall. Tom, Drake and the rest were on their way down toward my end of the hall. We gave a quick nod of greeting as we made our way outside and over to the post office. Gomez was inside holding a cup of instant coffee and standing behind the kid at the radio. He glanced over at me with a concerned look on his face. "I got reports of movement from the outer sentries. Looks like a couple squads out near the road where Alpha came in from earlier," he said.

"Yep, they're looking for their guys alright," Drake muttered.

"Guess we get to go play in the woods again then," I said.

"Brett said he wanted to see you Mack. He also said that you were to not go anywhere until you saw him," Gomez said.

I stood there, trying to control myself enough to not flip out on Gomez, when Drake put a hand on my shoulder and said, "It's ok bro, we got this one, you go see what he's all pissy about."

I clenched my teeth and nodded slowly, trying to let the anger pass. I heard Drake and Alpha leave. It took almost a minute before I could look at Gomez. "He's downstairs, and don't worry, there's gonna be a bunch of other teams out there, you won't be missing much," he said.

"I know, and thanks," I said as I gave him a weak smile and headed for the stairs. "You wanted to see me?" I asked as I walked through the door to the makeshift war room.

Brett sat in a chair at the table with a steaming cup of something along with Matt Wise and Mike Davids. "Yes Duncan I did. I mostly wanted to remind you that you can command troops from right upstairs in the communication center, so you don't have to go running around in the cold dark night. Secondly, I wanted to ask you if you've heard from Chris yet about the wounded?" he asked before sipping at his tea.

"No, I haven't. I'm assuming that they're okay for now. I'll go check on them at sun up," I said.

"Excellent, any word on what's going on out there now?" he asked.

"Couple patrols looking for their lost men we believe. I'm gonna go upstairs and find out if my men are okay," I said as I turned and left without another word.

I got upstairs and grabbed a chair, pulling it over to the radio table. I told the kid that I wanted him to check in with every team out in the field, and to get me locations and reports as quick as possible. Gomez handed me a fresh mug of black coffee and it started once again.

It had been like this almost the whole trek down here. Alpha and the rest out in the field, while I sat in whatever communications shack we had, being miserable, listening to everyone else do all the hard work.

## Chapter 4

"The shelling seems to have stopped," Anne said as she walked into the post office. She was being shadowed by a very shaky looking Lily.

"Yeah, yeah it stopped when their troops got closer to town," I said, leaning back in my chair and rubbing my eyes. The patrols had been dealt with and turned back pretty quickly. Alpha and the other teams had stayed inside the tree line, laying down enough harassing fire that they turned around and went home for the night.

"She really dislikes the shelling," Anne said as she scratched behind the petite German shepherd's ears.

"Yeah I bet, I don't like it either," I said smiling at Lily, who trotted over and licked my face as I leaned down to greet her.

"Do we have any word from Chris and the others that are back at the new clinic?" Anne asked.

"None yet, I'm gonna head over there at first light, which is like twenty minutes. If you'd like, you and Miss Lily are welcome to join me," I said.

"Sure, that'd be great, the triage unit is all caught up so I'll head there and see if I can help. Lemme go grab my stuff and see if I can find Liam to let him know where I'm going. I'll meet you out front in a few," she said as she jogged out the front door. Lily circled my chair and planted herself behind it, grunting contentedly.

She quickly returned and the three of us started the short walk up to our hospital. It was less than half a mile away in an old hockey rink. It was large enough to house our wounded and had no road leading in from the rear, which made it easier to defend. It was very early in the morning and cold, but not unbearable. We kept a brisk pace with Lily weaving back and forth in front of us, investigating everything in our path. It didn't take us more than a few minutes to make the walk. I could see the building as we came around the bend in the road.

About a hundred yards out and Lily stopped short. Her head tilted, listening to something intently that our ears weren't sharp enough to catch. She spun in a tight circle, stopping abruptly, to stare at me while giving a whine. Suddenly, I heard it too. **"RUN!"** I yelled. Anne and Lily took off.

**"INCOMING!"** I screamed, running behind them toward the hospital.

I heard the shell coming in. The piercing whistle gave it away. I didn't hear it hit, or the explosion that always follows. Instead, I felt as if I was being shoved across the small street leading to the rink. It felt as if I was flying and being pushed at the same time. Then, I could feel the burning, searing pain in my back, just before I hit the pavement face first. The ringing in my ears was deafening and I shook my head hoping to clear it. I looked up and could see the ground around me exploding as other shells hit, but I couldn't hear them over the ringing. Everything was blurry and I tried desperately to push myself up off the ground.

I got up onto my knees, the burning in my back was excruciating. I heard a wooshing sound and my ears cleared. Just then, someone grabbed me by my collar and dragged me toward the door. I could hear the shouting and screams of pain all around me, but couldn't focus my eyes enough to tell what had happened. I tried to speak, but all that came out was a howl at the burning in my back and shoulders. I flailed up at the person who was still dragging me inside and I could hear a man's voice calmly telling me to "Please shut up general, we're gonna make sure you're okay."

**"JESUS!"** I heard Chris scream as someone grabbed my feet and threw me up on a table. **"WHAT THE FUCK HAPPENED?"** she yelled.

"Shell blew up too close to him, tossed him halfway across the lot," the man said, rolling me face down. "This is gonna hurt general, a lot," he said, as screaming pain shot up through my back, into my neck and popped my eyes open wide. I started to scream and had a leather belt shoved into my mouth as I opened it.

**"OH SWEET JESUS, GIVE HIM SOMETHING, FOR FUCK'S SAKE!"** Anne screamed. I could hear Lily barking and howling at all the noise.

"I don't have time. He'll be fine once I get the shrapnel out of his back. Someone, get that dog outta here!" he said, pulling the first piece of shrapnel out. My body relaxed for a minute and I reached to take the belt out from between my teeth. White hot pain shot back through me as he went digging for another piece. I bit down hard on the belt and dug my fingers into the edge of the table, trying desperately not to thrash around.

Chris had stepped in to assist the doc and I could feel Anne stroking my sweat soaked hair, trying to keep me calm. To be honest, it wasn't really helping. The second piece came out and I could breathe for a moment. All I could taste was leather and dirt. Anne leaned down and came into my blurry line of sight. She smiled weakly as she told me that there were only two pieces left and that I was gonna be fine.

"They're coming, and soon," I growled as I spit the belt out.

"Wait doc, hold on. What Mack?" Anne asked me, leaning in close.

"They're coming, you have to get men here. The shelling is to soften up the target. We are obviously, the target. Call Gomez and get men here now, or we're all dead," I said breathlessly.

**"OH SHIT!"** Anne said stuffing the belt back in my mouth. "Finish him up doc. We may have less time than you thought. I'm gonna call Gomez," she said, standing and leaving the room.

The doc resumed torturing me. The third piece came out easier than the first two and I was hoping the worst was over. I discovered how wrong I was, when he started on the fourth piece. It had gone deeper than the others. Thankfully, I passed out for a few minutes from the pain, while he finished removing it. I came to shortly, to see Chris. She smiled when she saw my eyes flutter open. "Hey hon, doc says he got them all, but that you really should be bedridden for a couple days," she said before giving me a soft kiss.

"I'm fine," I said as I tried to sit up. The pain took my breath away and I moaned.

"Relax hon give the Morphine a minute to kick in," she said.

"We may not have a minute!" I said, "How much did you give me?"

"It's not my first day on the job asshole!" she said sounding indignant, "I gave you enough to dull the pain, but you should definitely still be mobile,"

"Good, we need to go, all of us," I said, forcing myself to sit up.

"Too late for that," Anne said as she came over to us.

"Why?" I asked.

"The shelling has stopped and the guards outside said they think they saw movement coming from the main road," she said.

"That's good, that'll be the guys Gomez sent," I said, nodding to myself trying to clear my head a bit. The aching and throbbing in my back was still painful, but the Morphine was helping to keep it manageable.

"Mack, honey I didn't get through," she said, looking sad. "Gomez doesn't know we need help yet."

"Wow that news would've sucked much more without the Morphine. This shit is great!" I said, sounding like I'd had a few too many.

"Great, he's high," Anne said with a sigh.

"I may be high, but we still have work to do if they're coming," I said, trying to push myself off the table. Chris quickly shoved her tiny hand into my chest and kept me sitting there.

"You tell us what you need and we'll do it. Just because you're in charge doesn't mean you have to do everything. Just tell us what to do," Chris said.

We spent the next five minutes relaying orders and setting people up, as well as moving wounded to a safer area of the building. It wasn't great, but it was the best I could do being high and short on time. I slid slowly off the table and limped over to grab my AK that was leaning against the wall. I thought twice about sliding the rifle over my shoulder and chuckled at the thought of how much that would hurt, even with the Morphine.

Anne had gone to see if we had gotten through to Gomez and find me a new ear bud. Mine had been blown out of my head during the explosion. I was limping to the front doors, when I heard the first shots rattle off. We had two guards outside the building and I had found five more men to join them. Three were wounded, two were doctors, but they all volunteered and could use a rifle.

The building was an old ice rink. It had no windows, only one set of main doors and a tiny back door. It did have a loading dock, but that was around the side of the building away from the main road. If they wanted to get there, they had to go through us, which may or may not be easier than I'd have liked. We had ringed old cars and trucks around the front of it when we decided to use it as a field hospital. In a perfect world, it would have been sandbags, but you use what you can.

Anne ran by me with an M-16 and a couple other less wounded men just before I got to the door. I hadn't heard any shots for almost a minute. I grabbed the door handle and heard Chris behind me. "Where do you think you're going?" she asked.

"Outside to help," I said, turning to see her with her hands on her hips.

"Not without me you aren't," she said.

"That's what I like to hear, utter confidence in the face of imminent death," I said with a smile as she grabbed an MP-5 off the table near the door, "Wouldn't happen to have more Morphine would ya?"

"You can have more, if we survive," she said as she opened the door for me. I could hear small arms fire from across the lot where the first barrier was.

"How's it lookin' out here?" I asked

"It's going pretty shitty actually," I heard a voice in my ear say. "We'll have to fall back in a couple minutes, almost out of ammo."

"Do what you need to son, we'll be here," I winced a bit as Anne fired off a short burst.

"Why can't we get in touch with Gomez?" Chris asked, squatting down next to a car a few feet away.

"Not sure, but I'm gonna keep trying, now that I have an ear bud that works," I answered.

"Boss," I heard Gomez say. "I can hear you boss, we're just tied up here. Where are you?"

"I'm at the field unit. We could use a bunch of help," I said. I felt Anne grab my shoulder.

"What?" I asked, glancing over my shoulder.

"Our boys are falling back Mack," she said, pointing at the men running toward us.

**"COVERING FIRE!"** I yelled and the wounded stood to cover their friends, with a hail of bullets, until they were safely behind the cars as well.

"Boss, were getting nailed here as well. Alpha and the other teams have things kind of under control, but it may be a bit before I can get someone back there,"

"Copy that. Keep me posted. We'll try and hold them here," I said with a sigh.

"Happy hunting boss," Gomez said.

**"I GOT MOVEMENT!"** I heard from down the line and a couple men opened up over to my right.

"Coming over the car!" Anne said as she swung her rifle over and fired off three rounds.

I flipped the selector on my AK-47 and fired off a few rounds in the same direction. The morphine was making me slow. All I wanted to do was sit down. Chris opened up as well. We heard shouts all along the line now, of troops coming over or around the makeshift barrier we had put in place. After they saw the first few of their friends go down they held back behind the cars for a bit. It gave us time to change magazines and get our shit together. It didn't last long though. I had sat down and was trying to stay focused, when I heard someone yell **"SMOKE!"** I grunted and pulled myself up off the ground to peek over the top of the car I was behind. They had tossed smoke grenades into the middle of the lot and were waiting for them to billow out enough.

"Stay calm, they'll be coming soon. Everyone get ready, it's about to get shitty," I said calmly, even while I was saying it, I wondered why I sounded so distant.

I leaned on the hood of the car to steady my fire since everything was really blurry. I noticed Chris doing the same on the car next to me. "Hey," she said, glancing over at me, "In case this is it; I love you."

"I know," I said with a smirk.

"You wish you were Han Solo asshole," I heard Anne say next to me.

"I do," I said, nodding slowly.

**"HERE THEY COME!"** someone yelled out as I saw the first of the dark figures come through the smoke. I didn't wait for them to take shape, I just opened up and so did everyone else. It didn't stop all of them, but more than a dozen made it no closer to our position. The troops returned fire and kept our heads pinned down, while they regrouped. Moving a bit closer now, they took cover where they could and tried to whittle away at us.

"Gomez, how's it lookin?" I asked.

"Good actually boss. Alpha says the teams have the army withdrawing, but it'll be a few more minutes. They're down the road near the woods," he replied.

"Divert a couple teams back this way as soon as possible. It's looking like we're about to get overrun," I said.

I felt something whack me in the head and looked up. "Sorry," Anne said as she slammed a fresh magazine home, after dropping her empty one on my head.

31

The smoke had stopped billowing out of the grenades and sat heavily a dozen feet in front of us. There was a fresh round of shooting. I pulled Anne down behind the car, a second before, a bullet shattered what was left of the windshield. Chris yelped as she spun and dropped behind her car as well, **"HOW THE FUCK DO YOU DO THIS?"** she screamed as the rounds tore through the thin outer metal of the car. Lily skulked up behind Chris and huddled behind the car looking terrified.

"Same way you treat guys with their guts hanging out. Practice," I said as I grinned at her, stood quickly and unloaded half a clip before dropping back behind the vehicle.

**"FUCK THAT,"** she said, ducking around the front to lay down some fire, "I'll take bodies any day, this shit is nuts!"

"It's about to get worse," I said, peeking around the front end of the car to see the huge black shadow moving in the smoke. **"HERE THEY COME,"** I yelled as I stood to see the first wave burst through the edge of the smoke a mere ten feet away. Everyone sort of fired at once. With me being high, it all seemed to slow down. I watched a couple of my men go down and more than a dozen of theirs. The first troop hit the front of my car running, and I caught him under the chin with the wooden stock of my AK. Anne finished him off when she put three rounds in him screaming **"FUCK,"** repeatedly. She then jumped up on the hood of the car and sprayed the area Rambo style, yelling the whole time, until she was empty.

I glanced over at Chris and saw two guys lunging at her across the hood of her car. One of them had her by the shoulder, as slow as I was, I spun to help and watched as she drew the pistol that was tucked into her back and put two rounds in his chest. The second soldier swatted the pistol away. I lined him up, again, not quickly enough. Chris had pulled the knife strapped to her leg and had shoved it into his side. He flailed at it for a second, before Lily grabbed him by his harness and dragged him onto the ground. She proceeded to claw and bite at him, until she found purchase on his neck. She was shaking her head vigorously like she had caught a rabbit. Chris had picked up her pistol, pulled Lily off and put one in his head.

I heard a barking yelp and spun to see. Anne stumbled and fell after a soldier clubbed her with the butt end of his rifle. He had it raised above his head, working toward an over head blow. I yanked my pistol out of what was left of my harness and fired into his back. At almost the same time, Anne fired into his chest. He stood suspended for a moment with a stunned look on his face before falling almost directly on top of her. I held out a hand and pulled her back over the hood of the car, "Stay over this side," I growled. She nodded in agreement.

"Boss, can you hear me?" Gomez asked.

"Yeah, tell me something good please," I said as I unloaded my Sig, dropped the mag and slammed a fresh one home. Then I unloaded half of my rounds, into two guys heading straight at me.

"Two teams are heading to you now, should be there in under two minutes," he said.

"Copy that," I said with a sigh of relief.

"You okay?" Anne asked as she glanced over at me.

"Calvary is coming," I said, smiling weakly and standing to lean on the hood of the car. I was firing sparingly, because I only had a couple extra clips for the Sig on me.

"I'm empty. Do you have any clips?" Anne asked.

"Not for that," I said.

"Bah, fuck it," she said as she dropped her M-16 and drew her chrome .357 and a giant hunting knife. I had given it to her years ago as a gift. She jumped up on the hood of the car, and dove on to a soldier that was running straight at Chris. She dropped the pistol, but shoved the blade up under his ribcage and shanked him repeatedly, her long black ponytail dancing back and forth as she stabbed him over and over. Chris had been firing her pistol sparingly to conserve ammo, but she saw someone run up behind Anne to pull her off his buddy and put two rounds dead center of mass. He stumbled back a few steps and fell.

"Hold on Mack, we'll have you clear in a minute," I heard someone say in my ear. It sounded like Buck, but I wasn't sure. My head was still foggy from the drugs.

"Copy that," was all I could manage, as I helped Anne up. I fired off a few rounds as the troops started to turn when they heard my men behind them. The docs and the wounded heard it as well and cheered before they hopped over the cars and pressed the advantage on the retreating troops. I of course, stood there somewhat dazed, leaning against the hood of an old Ford, watching as my men routed the force that had nearly slaughtered us a few minutes ago. Anne started to chase them down, but she soon saw that our men had arrived and decided to come join me at the barrier of cars.

"You okay?" I asked, sounding monotone, even to myself.

"Yeah, he may have broken my face, but I can still move everything," she answered. She was right, her left cheek had swollen dramatically and had already started to bruise. I heard Chris murmuring and glanced over to check on her. She was sitting, holding Lily, who had her faced nuzzled into Chris' chest.

"You two okay?" I asked.

"Yeah, yeah she's okay. She was just tryin' to protect her momma is all," she said with a soft smile as she scratched behind her ears, "She's a good girl."

I smiled and looked up to see Buck and some others striding toward me. "Glad to see you're all okay," he said as he shook my hand.

"Yeah, we're all great. Well, they're okay. I'm great, cuz I'm still really fuckin' high," I said with a grin.

Neither Chris nor the doc let me oversee the clean-up. They dragged me back inside and went to work on my back, which had busted open in a few different places during the battle. The Morphine helped this time around though, and I barely felt a thing as they sewed me back up. They ordered me to stay inside and in the cot they had put me in. Eventually, the doc went back to deal with the newly wounded.

"You did good out there," I said to Chris who was sitting at the end of the cot.

"Thanks, hope I don't ever have to do it again," she mumbled.

"You okay?" I asked.

"Yeah, I just… I dunno, I always knew what you did, and God knows this wasn't my first fight. It just always messes with me for a few days. It makes me feel like I'm never fast enough or strong enough," she said with a sigh.

"Doing shifts at the clinic, usually does the same for me. I always feel inadequate when I'm done. We both make it through though hon, so I guess we can't be as bad as we think. We just have different things we're more comfortable with," I said as I took her hand. "So, I take it you don't wanna join one of the teams then?"

"Hell no, but thanks for the offer," she said. "By the way, I didn't tell you since everything went so crazy, but I have bad news for you hon."

"Oh?" I said, raising an eyebrow.

"He's still alive, I know you were almost rid of him, but it looks like he's gonna make it," she said with a sly smirk.

"He's alive!" I said, sitting up.

"Yep, you were right. He did have a very weak pulse. I just couldn't find it with all the shelling. He's still unconscious, but he should be fine," she said, leaning down and kissing me on the forehead.

"Wow, first the Morphine and now this, it's like Christmas!" I said, smiling wide.

"Yes dear, now get some rest," she said, standing. "God knows how long it'll be before they need you again."

I nodded numbly to myself, agreeing with her. My eyes closed and I was out before she even walked away.

## Chapter 5

I opened my eyes and everything was blurry. Someone was sitting in a chair next to my cot, "Oh, hon you didn't have to sit with me. I know you're busy with patients," I croaked.

"It's okay dear, I wasn't really all that busy," I heard a deep, man's voice say.

I sat bolt upright, "What the fuck?" I asked, blinking and rubbing my eyes. "Great, I'm dead, or I'm dreaming."

"You are sadly mistaken friend. Neither of us are dead and if me in a fluffy robe is what you dream about, then I think we need to seriously rethink our relationship," George said, smiling

"You're awake," I said.

"Yep, woke up a few hours ago. Docs said I have a serious concussion, but otherwise I'm good. 'Bout time you woke up, Chris says you been out for like twelve hours now," George said grinning at me.

"See, I told you he'd be okay," Chris said as she walked toward me with a wicked looking needle.

"You we're right," I said smiling.

"Wow that really is nice to hear once in awhile." She grinned at me and flicked the tip of the syringe.

"What's that for?" I asked.

"We're keeping you pumped full of drugs to make sure you stay put. I know otherwise you'd be up trying to do stuff and we need that not to happen," she said sticking the needle into my arm. I started to protest, right up until the drugs kicked in. Then, I sort of just mumbled to myself for a bit before everything went blurry again.

I remember bits and pieces of the next couple days, but from what I was told, they kept me pretty out of it until they were sure my back was healing up. Chris was right of course. I never would have taken it easy or let myself heal otherwise. I finally came out of the haze to see George once again sitting in the chair next to my cot. This time he wasn't wearing a fuzzy blue robe though. He was back in his usual black cargo pants and lightning bolt t-shirt, today's happened to be red. He was reading something in a manila folder. He grinned as he heard me stir. "Docs say you can get out of here today. I guess they're tired of your snoring," he said chuckling to himself.

"How long have you been here?" I croaked, my throat felt like it was full of sand.

"Been here most of the time, they wanted to keep me close by too and I figured they could use my cot," he said, tossing the folder onto my legs. "That'll get you up to date. Things calmed down a bit after the attack here."

"What about the shelling?" I asked.

"Hasn't been any in at least twenty four hours," he said with a shrug.

"Alright then, I guess it's time to get back to work," I said, tossing back the blanket and sitting up on the edge of the cot. I attempted to stand and had to pinwheel my arms to keep my balance. George grabbed the front of my shirt to help keep me upright. "Lil dizzy?" he asked.

"Slightly," I answered, shaking my head. It took me a bit longer to get dressed than I would like and tying my boots almost made me pass out. Seems I wasn't quite as healed up as I had thought. The docs told me to take it easy for a few days while George stood behind me trying to stifle his laughter. They didn't seem to find it as amusing as I, or he did. Chris stubbornly gave her assent to me leaving the safety of the hospital and swore she was going to keep an eye on me. I smiled and gave her a grateful, "Yes dear," as I kissed her on the forehead. George and I headed back to the central command of the post office.

Gomez started a slow clap for the two of us, as we walked in. It was quickly picked up by everyone in the communications center. We both gave a little princess wave and made our way down the marble steps. Brett, Hags and some of the others were in the war room, discussing something that I'm sure they thought was incredibly important. That ended, as soon as they heard the door close behind us. After that, there was much rejoicing at the fact that we were both up and about.

They spent the next half hour or so, catching me up on just about everything that was in the folder George had tossed at me earlier. They seemed so happy though, that I didn't have the heart to tell them that I had already known all of the information they had just given me. Once I was finally caught up, we began talking about how to proceed forward. We were going to be in big trouble if we were stranded here much longer. We only had so many supplies with us. Drake had a plan to get us into the city and it seemed plausible. He had discussed it with Brett and Hags while I was out of commission, but they hadn't acted on it yet.

We went over the particulars of the plan briefly, and I decided that we would tell Drake to start putting together the mission. A short time later Gomez came into the room, "You should all really come upstairs," he said cryptically.

We glanced at each other around the room and followed him silently. Gomez wasn't one to play games like this and we all knew it. He walked us over to the communications equipment and picked up the radio. "Go again Echo," he said into the microphone.

"I say again, I have what looks like a female civilian that says she's here to help and would like to talk to someone in charge, copy," Echo said.

Gomez glanced over at me with a questioning look, "Whatta ya think boss?" he asked.

"Have one of Echo bring her in I guess. How much damage can one person do?" I asked with a shrug.

Gomez relayed my orders, "Looks like we're having company," I said as I took a seat to wait for Echo and our mystery guest to arrive.

It didn't take too long for them to get to the post office. According to what I'd heard later, she had walked right up to the guards we had posted with her hands above her head, to show she wasn't a threat. She was a taller woman, about five foot eight, thin and very in shape from what I could tell. She was pretty, but not in a cute way, she was more exotic looking. She had on a long black coat and matching black suede, no heeled boots. Her long dark hair was tied back in a ponytail that bobbed back and forth as she walked in.

"Hello, I'm Brett Twombly and you are?" Brett said as he shook hands with the lady.

"My name is Stacey, my boss sent me here to help you," she said with a smile.

"Alone?" Mike Davids asked. "There are an awful lot of troops out there."

"Well, as you can see, I got here just fine," she said, crossing her arms across her chest.

"Which would probably be why your boss sent you, instead of someone else," I said nodding slowly.

"Exactly," she said.

"Gentlemen, why don't we take our guest downstairs and have a bit of a chat," I said, smiling at Stacey.

They all murmured in agreement and we made our way back downstairs with our new friend. Once we were settled in, she told us that she lived in New York City proper and that the people there have been trying to get rid of the military for over two years with only partial success. Her boss was the main person in control of most of the city from what she said. He had been hearing the shelling for days, but knew it wasn't any of his people getting hit. Eventually, he figured out where we were and had sent her to meet us, in hopes that we could help get rid of the military once and for all.

"How'd you get past the troops?" Brett asked.

"One person is much harder to find than a large group," she said with a shrug.

"How're we gonna get into the city, we've already been pushed back once," Hags said.

"Because of the shelling correct?" she asked with a raised eyebrow.

"Yeah," he answered.

"Do you hear any shelling going on?" she asked again.

"No, but that doesn't mean anything," Brett said sounding annoyed.

"Actually, it does. I took care of the artillery problem on my way in." she said, checking out her fingernails.

"And how did you do that?" I asked.

"I'm a very resourceful woman. Besides, there were only three cannons aimed at you and each one is manned with five guys, so it wasn't all that difficult," she shrugged.

"I find that rather hard to believe," Brett said.

"I don't really care if you believe it. The shelling has stopped and in a few days you'll figure out that it isn't going to return and come marching through what few troops are left on this border of town. Either way, you'll get into the city. Might just take a couple extra days if you're stupid," she replied.

"Excuse me?" Brett said standing up.

"I'm quite sure you heard me. Yes, I said you're being stupid, get over it. I was sent here to help and I have. If you choose not to believe me, well, I can't really fix that can I?" she said calmly.

"Wait you killed fifteen men and you're unarmed?" I asked.

"Who said I was unarmed?" she answered with a smirk.

"Well Echo didn't hand over any weapons," Hags said.

"They didn't check for any," she said, sliding a long dagger out from the sleeve of her coat.

**"JESUS! WHAT THE FUCK?"** Hags yelled.

"Are you kidding me? No one checked you for weapons? Oh, for fucks sake!" I said as I grabbed it out of her hand.

"That's okay I have a few more, you can keep that," she said with a wink. "Listen, I came here to help, of course I'm armed, but I'm not here to kill any of you."

"Okay, everybody calm down. Mack and I will deal with the incompetence of Echo team and as for the cannon batteries; that is easily verified. We send a couple guys from Alpha with her to check out her information. Meanwhile, we make ready to move, so that by the time they get back we can start rolling. We don't wanna wait too long on this. They may discover they have a hole and plug it before we get there," George said.

"He has a very good point," I agreed. "Have Gomez get Drake and Tom. Have them come here ready to travel," I told the door guard who gave me a nod and jogged up stairs to the communications room.

"Duncan, can we talk to you for a moment, outside?" Brett said as he and Hags came to the door.

"Of course," I answered and stepped outside.

"So, you're the big man in charge," I heard Stacey mumble.

Brett closed the door behind us looking worried, "Do you really think we can trust her?" he asked me with a hiss.

"Probably not," I said with a shrug.

"So you're just gonna send Drake and Tom into a trap?" he asked.

"Well, it wouldn't be the first time I've done that, but no. If it smells bad Drake or Tom will catch a whiff and bail. They'll be fine," I said with a smile.

"That's a lot to trust to instinct," Brett said.

"It's gotten us this far," I said, clapping him on the shoulder and went back into the room.

"A couple of our men will escort you back to the cannon sites to verify your statements. Can I get you some coffee in the meantime?" I said as I walked by the chair she was sitting in.

"Real?" she asked excitedly.

"Instant, unfortunately," I answered.

"No thanks," she said pouting.

"I feel the same way," I said, pouring myself a cup of hot water to make a cup anyway.

Within a few minutes, Drake and Tom were ready to go. I had engaged our new friend in small talk, trying to glean a little bit of new information and failed miserably. She mostly kept her answers short, barely more than yes or no. Once or twice, I think she caught on to what I was trying to do and grinned like a Cheshire cat at whatever question I had just asked. She stood quickly and introduced herself to Tom and Drake. The three shook hands and then both looked at me waiting for an explanation.

"You're gonna go with Miss Stacey here and verify that the cannon teams are indeed taken out and that we should be able to get our men through with little resistance," I said, sipping at my coffee.

"That's it?" Drake asked.

"That's it. Don't engage anyone, don't try and take out any troops you may find. I want you three to just go in and then out. Is that clear?" I asked them.

"Crystal," Tom said.

"Good, call in when you get back into range. We'll be getting everyone else ready to move," I said with a nod.

"We'll be back lickity split," Drake said, waving over his shoulder as the three of them went out the door.

"No, you can't go. You still have stitches in your back," George said as he walked up next to me and crossed his arms across his chest.

"Was it that obvious?" I asked.

"It looked like it physically hurt when he turned around to leave," he said, nodding.

"Just a bit," I added.

"We need you here…" Brett started to say, before I held up a hand to stop him.

"Okay, before we go one step further, we have to have a discussion. Actually, it's going to be more of me talking and the rest of you listening," I said.

I heard George say, "Uh oh, here we go," as he sat at the table.

"I may be the commander of our forces and I may be part of the leadership structure of our little government, even against my better judgment, but I'm done with this staying back safe behind the lines. I

41

played it your way for a bit and got blown up because of it. From now on we do things my way. I will still be in command and still take care of all that needs taking care of. Now that George is back and somewhat healthy I'll be relying more on him, like I did back in Boston," I looked around. Brett seemed particularly annoyed and Hags was just nodding slightly. "Are we all clear about how this is gonna go now?" I asked.

"Yes, I understand, but I have to say that I disagree and think you should reconsider. We really need you here and safe," Brett said.

"Yup, heard it before, didn't like it then, don't like it now," I said, flashing Brett two thumbs up. His look went from annoyed to furious, but he held his tongue.

George and I took a ride out to have some very choice words with the members of Echo team. Gomez was in charge of Echo, but he spent almost all his time in the communications center. Once we were done with the ass reaming, the next couple hours were spent sending runners to the men telling them it was time to pack up. George and I wandered around our makeshift camp making sure preparations were underway. "So, you're gonna be rejoining Alpha I take it?" he asked as we came out of the triage unit.

"Yep, more than likely," I said with a shrug as we walked toward the barracks building. "We'll run things the way we used to. It'll be fine."

"Can't be any worse than it was before... have you mentioned this to Chris yet?" he asked with a raised eyebrow.

"Umm, nope," I said, scratching at my neck.

"Oh, please make sure I'm there when you do. There should be someone there to witness your final demise," he said with a chuckle.

"It won't be that bad," I said as he held the door open for me to go inside.

"Yeah, yeah it will," he said, sniggering behind me.

We got upstairs to find most of the troops were just about to start loading their gear out to the staging area. The trucks were already waiting outside. We made our way down to where Alpha was staying and found Jim, Eric and Woodsie packing the last of their stuff. I gave the boys a nod and ducked into Drakes room. He was bunking with Tom. I grabbed their duffel bags out from under the bed as George started to get their clothes off the floor. It only took us a couple minutes to get their gear together. I stepped out in the hall where Eric smiled and took Tom's bag off my shoulder as he passed me with his.

"I'll take that down to the truck boss," he said as he continued his way.

"Thanks," I said, glancing over at George.

"He's a good kid and helpful," he said with a shrug.

We were all outside by the trucks and I watched as the teams trickled down to load their stuff. After about a half hour the sentry at the door gave me an all clear of that building. George and I headed back over to the communication center at the post office to see if there had been any word from Drake. The rest of Alpha came with us and I filled them in on the way over about how I was rejoining their team. At first, Woodsie seemed a bit apprehensive, but after I assured him that no one was being dropped to make room for me, he perked right up.

There was a flurry of activity as we walked inside the old building. Gomez had most of our equipment broken down and there were a line of people carrying stuff out the door. Woodsie stayed behind to hold the door for a few people with heavier looking stuff. "I take it we've heard from Drake?" I asked Gomez as I came up behind him.

"Yeah, he gave us the all clear boss. He's on his way back with Tom and the girl. I'm breaking all this down, should be done in under ten minutes. He should be reachable by ear bud at this point, if you need to talk to him. Oh, and I'm really sorry. I heard about my team being stupid." Gomez grabbed a piece of equipment off the long folding table and spun around me as he took it outside to the truck.

I reached into my shirt pocket and popped my ear bud in as I went down the marble stairs. Roy and Brett were gathering up the last of the files and maps of the area that we had been using the last few days. Roy gave me a nod as he walked by with a box full of stuff. "They're on their way back and they said we're good to go," I told Brett.

"Excellent, let's finish this up and get moving then. We've been here too long." Brett rushed by me with another box and I checked the room to make sure we had everything.

Once we had the gear stowed away, it didn't take us long to get ready to move out. George and I were in the van carrying most of the communications equipment. We had taken out the back row of seats, so there was plenty of room for cargo. We had Chris, Eva, Sam, and Lily with us. Anne and Liam were driving Drakes car behind us. We were at the back of the line since we were carrying mostly non combatants. The side door slid open and Drake was standing there with Tom and Stacey behind him. "Hey boss, Got any room for us?" Not waiting for an answer he climbed in and took the seat behind me.

"How'd it look?" I asked while we waited for the last of our trucks to get into position.

"It looked great actually. She was dead on, three howitzer sites, all empty and deserted. We saw only a small force on our way back. It couldn't have been more than a dozen men." Drake said, scratching his heavy scruff.

"Excellent, shouldn't be any problem at all then," George said as he pulled forward slightly. The convoy was ready to roll it seemed.

"Did you tell Gomez?" I asked.

"Yep, he wanted me to let you know we were just about ready to roll. Seems kind of redundant now though since we are rolling," Drake said with a shrug.

It was late afternoon when the convoy really started moving along. I was looking out the front windshield watching the landscape roll slowly by us as we drove along. We were on the coast, but there didn't seem to be nearly as much destruction that there was up in Boston. It may have been because this stretch was inland and had more cover from the worst effects of the earthquakes that were set off after the storm. It was grey and overcast, the same as it always was. I was hoping we could get into the city proper and find a safe place to set up before nightfall. We weren't far out of the city, but we still didn't know what we were up against yet.

George was right when he said we'd have no problem with the troops. They had obviously heard us coming, because there was no one at the blockade when we got there. Being at the back of the convoy we wouldn't have even noticed that we had come to the barricade if it hadn't been for Gomez calling me to tell me that it was clear. It had been set up in the middle of a place called New Rochelle and once it was gone we rolled down Route 1 with no problem and into the city itself.

Once in, we continued down route 1, which oddly enough is called Boston Road according to Stacey. It took a bit of work, but we found someplace to set up shop for the night. It was long past dark by the time we came to the wide open area near the road we were on. It was an old football field next to a place called Seton Falls Park. It was going to be our campground for the night. We parked the vehicles in three circles like the wagons of the old west, and set about to feeding all the troops and setting up security. We had been at this for a couple months now, so setting up a new camp had become second nature.

I had walked the perimeter of our camp once everyone was settled in and saw that it was secure. After that was a quick check in with Brett, Hags and the other clan heads that were with us. By the time that was over, it was getting on in the night. I strolled back toward the van that George and the others were camped at. It was getting cold and I couldn't wait to get back to the fire. I never liked the cold, even less so now that I was old. Well, old in my opinion anyway. Everything ached and I had sharp pain shooting down my fingers from the biting chill.

The old white van was parked with its' doors in toward the fire and they were both swung wide open. George was curled up in the driver's seat, his sleeping bag tucked up under his chin, snoring away while Tom was on the passenger side with his up over his head, probably to block out some of the snoring. Small tents were set up around the fire. They all had portable heaters that ran off of small generators that we had brought with us. George and Tom hated being warm when they slept, so they tended to stay in the van with just enough heat coming off the large fires we would build. The only exceptions being the nights that it snowed, or when George had something with beans in it.

I smiled to myself and sat between the two doors to enjoy a bit of warmth from the fire. My hands finally started to feel better, after a couple minutes of holding them a foot or so from the flame. I was lost in thought, hearing only the crackle of the dried wood as it burned.

"Does he ever shut up?" I heard from behind me, making me jump slightly.

"Only when he stops breathing and then it's only for a short time and usually louder after," I answered. It was Stacey who was inquiring. They had given her a sleeping bag and blankets, but no one knew her well enough to invite her into a tent.

"Might not be such a short time if I have to listen to it too much longer," she grumbled.

I chuckled to myself. "Since you're up, wanna tell me how you killed fifteen men by yourself?"

"It's not like they were all together. Each battery had three guys running it and two guards. I separated the guards and took them out

45

one at a time. The others were a little tougher, but not by much. Usually the first was a surprise, that left only two at each site and two is easy," she said before she sat up.

"Still not the easiest of tricks," I said, rubbing my gloved hands together.

"Not my hardest by far," she said, unzipping her sleeping bag and coming down to join me between the doors.

"So, I take it, stuff like this is your job?" I asked.

"Among other things," she grinned wickedly. "I fill a number of roles for my boss. I'm like his right hand man, so to speak," she chuckled softly.

"Yes, your boss, what was his name?" I asked glancing over at her.

"Oh, didn't I tell you his name already?" she asked.

"No, no you hadn't mentioned it," I replied.

"Hmm, I thought I had. I'll have to remember to mention it sometime," she said, tapping her chin and staring into the fire.

"You could mention it now. You've been pretty tight lipped so far. A little info might make it easier to trust you,"

"Tight lipped me? You don't know me too well yet do you?" she said, grinning as she looked away from me.

"So, you're just gonna expect us to wander along with no information whatsoever?" I asked.

"Relax Mack, everything is going to be fine. We really are on the same side here. I was just playing with you a bit. My bosses name is Randall Riley, and he's a really nice guy," she said, shrugging.

"Thank you, that makes me feel much better," I said, feeling very relieved actually.

"Glad I could help make you…feel good," she flashed a quick grin as she slid back up onto the bench seat and zipped her sleeping back up. "G'night Mack, sleep sweet," she said as she rolled over.

I shook my head, smiled and stood. I paused by the fire, enjoying the heat radiating off of it, for another minute or so before I ducked into the tent and the sleeping bags that I shared with Chris.

## Chapter 6

We started out early the next day, just after sunup. Drake and I set out a few patrols to see if the locals were friendly, or if there were any locals for that matter. After a quick breakfast and some coffee to warm me up a bit, I checked in with George to let him know we were leaving. We jumped into Drake's car with Stacey. The rest of Alpha piled into Roy's pickup, that he so graciously leant to Tom for our little trip. Granted, he only leant it to him after Tom swore not to hurt the truck in any way, as well promising to take a bullet for the truck if the need arose.

George would tell Chris, Anne and the others where we had gone a little later on. I really wasn't in the mood to argue about my back not being healed enough. We rode slowly down route one. A few minutes down the road the heat kicked in and shortly thereafter I could feel the tips of my fingers again. Drake glanced over at me and asked where we were heading. I in turn glanced over my shoulder at Stacey and asked the same question. "I have no idea where you're heading. I'm just here because you told me to get in," she said smiling.

"Okay, how about, take us to your leader," I said, grinning.

"Ah, well that I can do. Head toward Grand Central Station," she said.

"Wait, that can't be right. We were told the military controlled Grand Central," I said, spinning around in my seat to face her.

"They DID," she said, nodding, "That was over a year ago though. Now, they mostly stay to the borderlands."

"Borderlands?" I asked, calming down a bit.

"Like I said, we've been trying to get rid of them for over two years now. At this point, they mostly just stay along the edges of the city keeping us in here. There aren't enough of them to surround us, so they just keep the exits out of the city locked down," she said with a shrug.

"So, you're free to roam around as long as you stay in the city. Sort of like being stranded on an island, or in a prison," Drake said.

"Yep, which is just another reason to get rid of them," she agreed.

"So, your people are based out of there now?" I asked.

"Seemed fitting," Stacey answered.

"It does make sense," Drake said.

"Okay, well I guess that's your answer then. Head to Grand Central Station," I said.

Things were quiet and deserted on the outskirts of the city. Once we got a bit deeper in, that started to change. Even though it was still early in the day, we saw small clusters of people walking around. Some were carrying empty baskets and some full. When I asked Stacey, she told me that they were either going to, or coming from their food distribution area. She said it was always better to get there early because they only brought so much in every day and it went fast.

We were getting the hairy eyeball from almost everyone we passed, since we were the only vehicle we saw that was in one piece. There were parts of cars everywhere, but it looked to me that everything of use had been picked off of them years earlier. Stacey explained that every neighborhood had their own "store" for food and other goods so there wasn't really a need for cars. It also allowed the gas to be used for more important things, like the generators.

We got to a turn in the road that would lead us over a small bridge and into Harlem. Stacey told Drake to stop where we were and to NOT go over the bridge. She got out of the car and hopped up onto the back trunk. She reached into her coat and pulled out a small radio. I joined her at the back end of the car, listening as she talked to someone at the other end of that radio. He told her to stay where she was and that someone would be out soon to meet with us. She let them know that she had heard and would be waiting. "You heard the man," she said as she climbed in the back seat.

"Why do we have to wait here?" Drake asked.

"Probably the same reason why he got so mad that no one frisked me," she said, pointing at me.

"Yeah, I can't say I blame them for not trusting us," I said.

It wasn't long before we saw a couple cars coming toward us from deeper in the city. The lead car stopped about thirty yards away from us and parked lengthwise across the street. The second car was directly behind it and had blacked out windows. I was sitting on the hood of our car with Drake. The rest of Alpha waited in the bed of Roy's pick-up with Eric sitting on the tailgate, his M-16 strapped to his back. Stacey was leaning on the side panel of Drake's car, filing an edge off of one of her nails.

I saw the passenger side and back door open on the second car and watched as two men got out. The first guy I saw was definitely a bodyguard. He was tall, jacked and just screamed mean. He was wearing black combat boots with black jeans, a well worn, dark brown leather jacket, a Scali cap, and looked like his nose had been broken, more than a couple times. In his hand he was carrying a shiny, chrome desert eagle, which I'm sure wasn't just for decoration.

The second gentleman was smaller of build and lean. He was wearing black cowboy boots, and a long black leather trench coat. He was bald and had on what would have been a pretty expensive pair of Oakley sunglasses, back in the day. He saw Stacey and smiled as he walked toward us. I watched, as his bodyguard took stock of everything and everyone in the immediate area. He was wary, but not overly so. The "Boss" gave Stacey a big hug and a quick kiss before any other business.

"Good afternoon gentlemen," he said, flashing a very wide smile.

"Boss, this is Duncan Mackenzie, Mr. Mackenzie this is my boss Randall Riley," Stacey said as he reached out and shook my hand with a solid grip. "Nice to meet you, glad you're here," Randall said.

"You as well," I said with a nod and a smile.

"Friends call me Riley Mr. Mackenzie," Riley said as he pulled out something that resembled a cigarette.

"Mine call me Mack," I watched as he pulled out a black Zippo and lit the tip.

"Mack it is," he said with a nod and a large exhale of something that definitely smelled like tobacco.

"You have smokes?" Drake said from the hood of his car.

"I do indeed," Riley said, smiling. He was still wearing the triangular sunglasses. They made him look like a Jack O'lantern with all the smiling. "You don't?"

"No, unfortunately," I sighed.

"My mama taught me not to be a quitter. I sure as hell wasn't gonna let the end of the world stop me. So now, I grow my own," he said with a shrug.

"I kinda figured feeding whoever was left was a better idea in our case. We didn't have a lot of room for growing," I said, trying to defend our lack of luxury.

"Here, have a couple on me. I've got plenty," he said, tossing me the cigarette case.

"Thanks," I said as he held out the lit Zippo for me to light one. I tossed the case to Drake and he took one before passing it around. Soon, all of Alpha was having their first smoke in quite a long time. Some were enjoying it more than other. I was most assuredly one of the enjoyers.

I was a long time smoker and the first year after the storm was incredibly hard. Torn between a habit I enjoyed and trying to stay alive after twenty odd years of smoking wasn't easy. Add to that, the fact that there were soon no tobacco products to be had and it got even harder. Thankfully, there were a lot of things to keep me preoccupied while I dried out. Looking for food, medicine and just trying to survive in general to name a few.

The smokes made for an, almost instantly, relaxed atmosphere. Riley gave us a minute to enjoy them before he started to speak, "I really am glad you boys are here," he said, "Maybe now we can get rid of these fucks once and for all."

"We'd be glad to help, especially if you can keep their big guns quiet as well as you did the ones that drove us back the first time," I said drawing some of the sweet smoke into my lungs.

"I'm sure together we can do any number of things. How many men did you say you had with you?" he asked.

"Two thousand, or so," I answered.

"EXCELLENT! We'll be free of these bastards in no time!" Riley exclaimed.

"Stacey, where are they camped?" he asked.

"They're up at Seton Falls Park right now," she said.

"That's no good at all. We need to get you all much closer to us. Stacey here will be our liaison. I need her for a few hours, but we'll send her up to meet you later on today and see about finding a more suitable place for you to camp here in the city proper," Riley said as he flicked his cigarette into the road.

"That sounds great," I said with a small smile.

"Outstanding," was all he said as he took Stacey by the hand and pulled her closer to him. "Again it was great to meet you and I am truly thankful that you're here. I think this is going to be beneficial for both of us."

"Pleasure to meet you as well, Riley," I said. I heard Tom and the others piling into the pick-up, leaving Drake and I leaning against the hood of his Monte Carlo.

"You gonna be okay to get back to your men?" he asked, standing behind the open door of his car.

"Oh yeah, of course, we're fine," I said with a dismissive wave.

"I'll have her back to you later today then. Look for her around two or three," he said, giving us a wave and disappearing inside. His car turned, and in under a minute was out of sight.

"Well, that was…interesting," Drake said as we stared off at nothing.

"No shit huh." I said. We glanced at each other and shrugged before we got back into the Monte.

We talked on the ride back to the camp and realized that both of us had a bad feeling about Mr. Riley. Neither of us could quite put a finger on it, but we had both learned in our relative old age to trust our guts. Right this moment, our collective gut was pretty sure something wasn't right. Drake thought it could be something as simple as the fact that Riley wouldn't trust us yet either, and he'd keep things close to his chest. I agreed that it COULD be that simple, but part of me didn't think so.

On our way through the Bronx, I saw that some of the side roads had makeshift barricades on them. They were just two cars parked end to end, effectively blocking off the smaller streets. Some of them were manned, most were not. The ones that were manned had at least two people, armed with assault rifles. They seemed to be watching the main street that we were on. They didn't do anything as we passed by, but they had definitely noticed us. As we left the Bronx, I noticed that there were four cars, two parked on each side of the street across from each other. I figured they were the movable barrier for this main street here. They were the only four in the area that had an engine, much less tires.

I wasn't sure why it gave me an uneasy feeling, I mean we had similar defenses set up back home. I think it was Riley's laid back friendly attitude, mixed with barricades and assault rifles that didn't sit well. Nothing I could really do about it now, but I did take notice of where they were and pointed them out to Drake as well. He just nodded and said that he had seen them as well.

It was barely ten AM when we got back to camp. We made our way straight to George's van and parked outside of the ring. George was still sitting in between the open cargo doors, warming his hands. Anne, Eva and Chris were sitting next to the fire drinking something, probably coffee. Lily was curled up on one of the bench seats inside the van. Sam was in the row behind her, I guess being pregnant and all, it wasn't very comfortable for her on the ground.

"Well, nice of you to finally show up," Chris said, barely glancing up at me.

"Told you she'd be mad," George snickered. He shrugged off the blanket he had wrapped around his shoulder, reached into his sweatpants pocket and pulled out an individually wrapped Twinkie. It was a bit smushed, but still looks intact. He smiled wide as he pulled off the wrapper and shoved half of it in his mouth. "Breakfast of champions!" he exclaimed with some of the creamy filling on the corners of his mouth.

"I am not mad, and how long has that been in your pocket?" Chris asked. "Beats me," George said, pulling the blanket back over his shoulder. The Twinkie was now gone. "If Mack wants to do something stupid that's his choice, he's a grown man, he just acts like a stubborn child,"

"See, she's not mad," Eva said with a big smile.

"Obviously," I said, rolling my eyes and taking a seat next to my not angry wife.

"Where'd that Stacey chick go?" George asked, finally wiping the filling off of his mouth.

"She'll be back later today, at least, that's what her boss said," Drake said as he climbed by George, to go sit with Sam inside.

"Good, I think I'm gonna tap that," George said while making a spanking motion with his right hand.

"Uh huh," Anne said, shaking her head.

"What? I think I got a shot. It Isn't like I have all that much competition these days. I even have my hair still," he said combing his fingers through it.

"Some of it, anyway," Drake said from behind him.

"Stuff it Goldilocks, no one's got more hair than you I know, but still," he said.

"You know she killed fifteen men the other day, right?" Anne asked.

"Oh I know, wicked hot isn't it?" George asked excitedly.

"Ten bucks says she slits his throat the first time he swats her ass. You know he's gonna try it at least once," Drake snickered.

"Too true," I said, nodding as I poured hot water from the kettle that had been hanging over the fire, into a cup.

Drake and I then filled George in on the meeting we had just had with our new friend and ally Mr. Riley. It didn't take too long, and at the end of it, George agreed that something didn't smell right. We also told him about the blockades we saw in town After a few moments pondering, he had decided to leave that on a back burner. Eventually, Chris softened when she realized that all I had done was go for a drive. She still didn't like the idea of me throwing myself back into harm's way. Drake assured her that he would keep an eye on the old man with a smirk, which I don't think made her feel any better about it.

Chris leaned over and gave me a quick kiss before getting up. I heard her make a sound and I glanced up at her. "Yeah, I didn't miss the taste of cigarettes over the last five years. You're not gonna start smoking again are you?" she asked.

"No hon, not at all. It just would've been rude to not have one is all," I answered.

"True, I suppose. No more though okay? They really do taste gross," she said with a smile and a wave. "Off to go check on patients, be back a little later."

"Of course not, see you in a bit," I said, smiling and waving as she made her way out of sight.

"You're so lying to the poor girl," Anne said with a grin.

"Of course I am," I smirked.

"I'm pretty sure everyone else here knew it too," George said while Drake just nodded.

"I'm betting SHE knew it too," Sam said from the bench seat.

"Yeah, she probably did, but I'll continue to have my self-delusion of being overly clever, if it's all the same to you," I said to her with a wink.

"I was just sayin'…" she said with a shrug and a smile.

"I suppose we should head over to the command tent and let them know how it went, and that we'll be moving later today," George said as he stood, stretched and tossed the blanket he had draped over his shoulders, into the front seat of the van.

"You make it sound like so much fun," I said as I got up and cracked my back.

"Y'know if you'd stayed here like you were supposed to, you could have made him go do it," George said hooking a thumb toward Drake. "Consider it penance for not doing what you're told."

"I'm not really religious, can't say I believe much in penance," I said as we walked away from the fire.

"You may not be religious Mack, but trust me, you are going to hell. You might wanna reconsider penance," he said, grinning.

Brett was incredibly curious about Mr. Riley. Our meeting had been so short though that I couldn't give him too much information, except a description and my gut reaction to him. He did like the idea of us being further into the city, and was hoping that they'd find a place that had a roof for us to call home for a short time. He did ask to be included in the next meeting I had with Riley. I told him of course, but that I had no idea when that would be.

George and I separated after that. He went to go get folks started on packing our gear up and I went to grab Drake to meet with the patrols that were either already back, or coming in soon. I only met with the patrol leaders, so that the other could grab some food and help with packing up. We found a quiet corner for them to give their reports. There wasn't anything too odd about them, they saw a few people about, and no one wanted to talk to them. The only little thing that stood out was that they all felt like they were being watched. If it had just been one, I may have dismissed it, but since it was all of them then it was more than likely true. Again, not really surprising, it was nice to know they all had good instincts.

A little before noon, Gomez came to find me, to let me know we were ready to go. It hadn't taken long at all, since we knew this was a temporary move. Stacey showed up just before two and told us that Riley had picked out a nice homey spot for us to park our asses for a while. We made the call and everyone loaded themselves up into whatever vehicle had room. Stacey rode in the Monte with Drake and I, I let her sit in front, so that she could tell us where we were going. The convoy formed up behind us, and shortly we were on our way. We made decent time and soon found ourselves pulling up in front of our new, temporary home. Stacey told me that it used to be Mt. Sinai Medical Center, and that the whole facility was at our disposal as long as we needed it. She also mentioned that Riley had made sure the heat and power worked. She didn't think the water was on, but that there was a reservoir nearby in Central Park.

I myself was stunned that this whole block had power and heat, according to what she said. Obviously, Riley had some kind of power plant set up. I couldn't figure out how he'd done it, but he had. Brett nearly broke into a dance when he found out that we had not only a roof, but heat and electricity as well. The troops were elated as we started moving all of our gear and people inside. We had been living like cave men compared to Riley and the people of New York I thought, as I walked up the stairs and inside the bright humming building.

Chris came and found me shortly after we arrived and kissed me hard on the lips. As I stood there shocked, she rambled about how some of the monitors and equipment still worked, and that she was so very happy, and couldn't wait to meet Mr. Riley, and thank him for such wonderful accommodations. Yes, she said it all in one very long breath. It was followed by another hard kiss before she skipped down the hallway, back to where her patients were.

## Chapter 7

The mood remained light, even hours later, when Riley showed up in a shiny black Cadillac. Most everyone was relaxing after one of the first hot, sit down meals we'd had in months. Riley had even left us fresh meat in the kitchen, along with some really tasty home brewed beer. The warmth that the heat provided felt incredible on my old bones after months of being on the road.

Some of us were sitting in the large main hallway, in a semicircle of large black leather chairs and couches. Brett, Hags and I sat in the three chairs. Drake and Chris claimed two separate ends of one of the couches and Eva and Teddy were curled up on the other. I saw Riley come in, preceded by his bodyguard. He was still wearing his long black leather coat and his smile grew large, as he saw that we seemed to be enjoying ourselves. I walked toward him in greeting and we stopped several feet from the cluster of seats.

"Hey there Riley," I said as I shook his hand.

"Hello there Mack," he said, grinning, "Here ya go, put these somewhere safe. Those are just for you." I looked down and he had palmed me a silver cigarette case. He tossed me a wink as I slid them into the pocket of my cargo pants. With a nod we walked together over to the others.

"For those of you that don't already know, this is Mr. Riley, the benefactor of tonight's meal and our host here in New York," I said as everyone stood.

Brett stepped forward and shook his hand, grinning ear to ear as he introduced himself, "Pleasure to meet you sir, I'm Brett Twombly, I just wanted to thank you for such wonderful accommodations." Riley gave him a "Nice to meet ya," as they shook.

"The food and heat were pretty kick ass as well," Hags said as he raised his beer bottle to Riley in salute. "That is John Hagerty, or Hags as we call him. He's the clan head of Boston proper," I said as Riley gave him a curt bow.

"This is one of our team leaders Ted…" Riley cut me off mid sentence and stepped by Teddy, who I was introducing. Riley stood staring at Eva, who suddenly started blushing at the attention. "Who is this exquisite creature?" Riley asked while removing his sunglasses and taking Eva's hand to plant a very soft kiss on the back of it.

"My name is Eva," she said with a small curtsy and a giggle.

"Of course it is, it fits you perfectly. Please forgive my being so forward. Seeing a beautiful girl isn't as common as it used to be," he said, his eyes still locked on hers. "Thank you," was the only response from the, fire engine red faced, girl as she slowly sat back down on the couch.

"I do apologize, Ted was it?" Riley said, moving to shake Ted's hand.

"No problem at all sir," he said, sitting back down on the couch. "I get distracted by her all the time."

"Oh, are you two a couple?" Riley asked, pointing back and forth between them.

"No, no, not at all, we're just old friends," Eva spoke up quickly.

"Good, I thought my world was about to end, again," he said with a wink toward her and put his glasses back on. "You sir, were at our first meeting, I believe," he said as he and Drake shook hands quickly.

"And last, but in no way least, is Christina, she's in charge of all our medical personnel and my wife," I said, directing him toward her.

"You better say that." She winked before shaking his hand. "I just wanted to thank you for the incredible hospitality sir. The fact that we have electricity and working medical equipment was amazing enough, but the food, beer, and heat on top of it, is just incredible, so thank you again," she said, smiling softly.

"You are all very welcome. Think of it as my way of thanking you for helping us free ourselves soon," he said, smiling at all of us.

"Please, sit and join us, we were just relaxing after dinner and enjoying being warm for a change," I said as everyone started to sit.

"Thank you, don't mind if I do. Oh, and speaking of keeping warm," he said sitting on the middle cushion of the couch between Eva and Teddy. He smiled and pulled a bottle of Johnny Walker Blue from out of his long black leather jacket.

"Jimmy, can you go grab us some glasses?" he asked as he pointed to his bodyguard. "This is Jimmy by the way, he's almost always with me and he'll be joining us as soon as he finds us something to drink out of." Jimmy wandered off toward the kitchen.

Jimmy came back shortly with as many glasses as he could find. It wasn't quite enough, but no one really minded sharing. We offered him a seat multiple times, but he refused with a soft smile as he stood silently behind his boss. Riley broke the seal and started pouring. He offered the first to Hags who looked as happy as a small child on Christmas morning. The next was offered to Brett who politely declined, since he didn't drink. I could swear I saw an instant of anger flash across Riley's face, but it was quickly restored to the big smile I was getting used to, when Hags joyfully stated, "Excellent, more for me then!" We all had a good laugh and soon everyone, but Brett had a glass of a very smooth whiskey in their possession. Even Chris, who was more of a rum fan, went back for seconds.

We sat and relaxed, talking long into the evening. Riley was supremely curious and had lots of questions. By the end, I'd say that he probably knew more about us and our command structure than I would have liked. George joined us later and brought one of our bottles of Maker's Mark once the bottle of Johnny Walker was gone. He was seriously perturbed at the fact that no one saved him any. By the end of the conversation, Riley and Eva were exchanging glances and secret little in-jokes. We were all very protective of her and I was curious to see how this new friendship was going to play out.

As the night grew late, several folks wandered off to get some well deserved rest. The few of us that remained included me, Hags, George and Brett. Of course Riley, and his bodyguard Jimmy, remained as well. Sam had come to drag Drake off well over an hour earlier. He had carried Chris off to tuck her in when he left. Teddy had thought it a smart idea to call it a night shortly after that, when he saw Riley edging closer to Eva on the couch. Teddy stood and held a hand out to Eva offering to walk her to her room. That was the second time I had seen a quick glimpse of Riley's anger. Eva giggled and accepted. She loved the attention she was getting from both men.

"Did you have a timetable for when you'd like to start pushing the military out?" Brett asked Riley.

"As soon as possible," he said, finishing off his drink before pouring himself another half a glass. "I've already put out the word to start gathering up my men."

"Do you have a head count?" I asked.

"I have about five hundred armed and trained," Riley said.

"Wow, that many just from the city?" I asked.

"We do have a much larger population then you do. Added to the fact that, from what you've told me, we didn't sustain a lot of the damage that you did," he said, and he was right. We had had a small meteor hit nearby that took out part of Boston, as well as the earthquakes from the offshore fault line. New York, being tucked further inland hadn't suffered as much destruction as we had. It was by no means untouched though. They had been hit by the earthquakes, but had from the looks of things, had only about half the amount of damage. Most of their losses were out in the Long Island area Riley had mentioned.

"Do we know how many troops they have?" George asked.

"My original count was around a thousand, but that was two years ago, before we drove them to the borderlands. I'm gonna guess around five hundred now," Riley said, nodding to himself. "They only have enough to cover the exits to the city nowadays."

"So, if we use a thousand of our troops we should be fine," George said, staring off at nothing, which he did a lot when he was thinking.

"Only a thousand?" Riley asked, sounding surprised.

"That would give us two to one odds, which should be plenty. They're more than likely, just as tired of this fight as you are. You have to remember, most of their troops are only in it for the free food and shelter. Once their command structure is cracked, they should fall apart," George said with a shrug.

"I know I should defer to you, since you've done this before," he said. "But I was wondering if it wouldn't be better to send in my men as well."

"I'm not sure we need that many," George said, scratching his chin.

"The reason I ask is this; one, my men know this city much better than yours do, which will make traveling much easier. Two is that it would boost my men's morale. You have to remember, these men have been trying to get rid of the army for two years now. If you come in and clear them out by yourselves, they'll feel like failures. That may not mean a lot to you, but I need those men to help defend this city after you leave," he said, looking solemn.

"Hmm, those are both good points," George said as he glanced at me.

"I see no reason not to take the extra help," I said with a shrug.

"Excellent!" Riley said. George shot me a dirty look and I shook him off until later. George rolled his eyes at me and drained his tumbler

"So, when will your men be ready?" Riley asked.

"If we work through tomorrow to get the teams set and figure out a plan, we can be ready to go as fast as the morning of the next day," I said, glancing over to George who gave a small nod.

Riley winced, "Make it two days, as much as I want to be rid of these pricks, I need the extra day to make sure my men know what they're doing," he said.

"That'd be fine, gives us more time to obsess about the details," George said, grinning. "No one else likes when Mack and I obsess, but we enjoy it."

We talked for another hour, or so before Hags let out a huge yawn and decided that he was all done. Brett quickly followed and Riley agreed that it was indeed getting late. He told us that he'd be in contact tomorrow and to let Stacey know that he'd need to see her sometime tomorrow as well. I said that I'd happily pass the message along, and that perhaps it was a good idea if I came down to his headquarters with her, so that I could get a peak at his operation as well. Riley assured me that we'd get to see Grand Central soon; but that he needed his people focused on the coming battle and that an impromptu visit probably wasn't a good idea. I gave a small smile and nod in agreement. Riley stood and stretched, clapped Jimmy on the shoulder as he said "Home James." I gave a small chuckle. Riley returned my laughter with a big shark like smile and nod, "Yes, that is exactly why I have Jimmy drive me around," he said as he strode toward the doors.

After the doors closed, George turned to me, his fake smiled dropped, "Care to tell me what the FUCK that was all about?" he asked.

"What?" I asked.

"We've never fought with his troops, why in God's name are we gonna mix them in with ours? That doesn't seem like a good idea at all," he said, fuming.

"We hadn't fought with the troops at the Mass Ave. Bridge either and that worked out fine," I said with a shrug.

"I thought you didn't trust him," he said.

"I don't, and we aren't going to mix our troops either. We'll send them in separately. We'll give them just enough to do to feel useful, but it'll still be our troops doing the heavy lifting," I said.

"I suppose that would be okay. I just don't know how much I like this idea," he said, pondering my plan.

"Pfft, it'll be fine," I said, waving him off.

"Other than his troops, this sounds like it should be simple," George said trying to drop the subject.

"What's he hiding at Grand Central?" I asked.

"I have no fucking idea, but he sure doesn't want us seeing it. Yeah, I caught that as well," George said scratching at the scruff on his chin. "I was trying to ignore it, but since you went and kicked the elephant in the room, right in the nuts, I guess I can't now, thanks."

"Sorry, didn't mean to piss on your happy parade," I said sighing.

"Oh, it was more of a denial parade actually. You ain't the only paranoid fucker in the room. I was just kinda hopin' we could get this done and go home not having to deal with it," he said, glancing at me.

"You really think that's gonna happen?" I asked incredulously.

"Nope, it never does," he sighed again.

I slept badly, if you could call it sleep. It was more like a lot of tossing and turning with intermittent mini dreams involving sharks. I gave up after awhile, and decided that coffee was necessary. It was early in the morning, people were just starting the day. Well, those of us that hadn't stayed up until four AM drinking were. I grabbed a mug and opened the spout on the large steel coffee urn. My nose caught a whiff of something strange and I glanced down into the porcelain mug. I nearly dropped it on the ground when I saw that there was actual coffee in my mug. "SWEET JESUS!" I exclaimed and I heard someone chuckle behind me. Gomez was standing there with a mug of his own. He took a small sip, "fucking awesome right? I had forgotten what real coffee had tasted like," he toasted me with the mug, turned and started walking to one of the tables talking to himself, "I wonder if he's married. I'm not gay, but if the man has real coffee every day, I could probably fake it for awhile."

I grabbed a second mug and filled it before heading out of the small cafeteria. I made my way down a long corridor to the room that Sam and Drake had settled into. Pushing down on the handle, I shoved the door open and slid inside. The lights were still off and I heard Sam, "Morning Mack," she said sitting up and scooting her back up against the headboard. She was very pregnant, but it didn't show as much as I thought it would by now. "Did you bring me coffee?" she asked, turning on the bedside light. She knew that I wouldn't have brought it for Drake, since he didn't drink coffee.

"Umm, no I didn't, but you can have this one," I said, holding out the mug in my left hand.

"Who's the second cup for then?" she asked.

"Me," I said with a shrug, "It's real; I didn't want them to run out before I got a second cup."

"Holy crap! It's real?" she asked as she held the mug under her nose and blinked a few times in disbelief.

"What's real?" I heard Drake ask sounding groggy, hidden almost completely under his blankets.

"Mack has real coffee!" Sam said.

"Not surprised," Drake grumbled, "The beer was real too."

"Maybe we should just stay here Mack, seems like they have a lot more stuff than we do,"

"A lot more luxury items yes. That's kinda why I'm here," I said.

"Why, what's up?" Drake asked as he sat up and stretched his arms up over his head. I could still see the puckered scar where he had been shot all those months ago at Fenway.

"Figured me and you would go for a little walk and see what's what," I said, sipping at my coffee. The full rich aroma hit my nose and I could swear I almost swooned in ecstasy.

"You got that itch don't ya?" he asked, his bleary, red rimmed eyes, glancing over at me.

"Yep," was all I said.

"Me too," he said, sliding down to the end of the bed and grabbing his black cargo pants. He pulled them up he sat in a chair near the door and started to put on his socks and boots.

Sam looked at us both incredulously as she held the warm mug under her nose. "What itch?" she asked.

"The itch means something ain't kosher," Drake started to explain as he finished tying the first boot. "It's that feeling that something's not right, but you don't know what it is. It feels like there's this itch at the base of your skull that you can't get rid of."

"You have these itches often?" Sam asked.

"All the time," we answered simultaneously before we busted out laughing.

"You two really should have been a couple," she said, rolling her eyes.

"Nah, it'd never work between us," I said, opening the door to the hallway.

"He's right," Drake said, tossing a t-shirt over his shoulder and leaning down to give Sam a quick kiss, "With that much sexy in one couple, we'd never do anything productive. Love you,"

"I'll have him back by dinner hon," I said with a smile and a wink.

"Bye," I heard her say as the door closed.

We walked down to the front of the building. I ducked in to refill my coffee, since I had given the second mug to Sam. Drake grabbed a couple pieces of what looked like toast made from thinly sliced homemade bread. He looked down at the small bowl next to the plate of toast, then over at me, "Dude, is that butter I'm looking at?" he asked, scooping some it up with the knife that was left next to it.

"You can't be serious," I asked, sliding up next to him. Watching, as he took a taste and blinked. "Wow, that is really and truly butter," he said, smearing a big pile of it onto the two pieces of bread.

"Something is seriously not right about this," I said as I grabbed two pieces for myself and coated them thickly with the butter.

"So, are we in the Matrix and we're actually being sucked dry of our energy in some weird cocoon?" he asked as we walked down the stone steps to the Monte.

"Dude, that is real butter and this is real coffee," I said, raising my mug, "So, yeah possibly."

"Cool, I'm Morpheus then, which I guess makes you Keanu," he chuckled as he popped the trunk to grab our gear.

"Why do you always get to be Morpheus?" I asked as I snapped my harness into place.

"Obviously because I'm cooler," Drake shrugged.

"But you're not black or older than me," I said, sliding my boot knife into place. "Nor are you bald either."

"I'm black from the waist down though, so I have to be Morpheus," he said, handing me my AK-47.

"Funny, to hear Sam tell it, your black Irish from the waist down," I said, sliding a mag into the rifle.

"Ow, nicely done," he said, pulling the long leather coat on, "Where the hell are we goin'?

"Thank you," I said, taking a quick bow, "I have no idea actually. I do know that we haven't done a decent recon since we've been in this city, and I don't like that at all. Let's head in the general direction of Grand Central and see what we can see."

"Lead the way Kemo Sabe," he said.

We turned to leave the Monte and I caught a glimpse of Stacey coming down the stairs toward us, "Hey, where are you boys off to?" she asked cordially.

"Just goin' for a morning walk is all," I answered, groaning internally.

"Cool, lemme just go grab my stuff," she said quickly turning around to go inside.

"No need, you stay here. We won't be too long," I said, trying to sound nonchalant.

"I REALLY think I should go with you. I am your liaison. It really wouldn't be good form for me to let you get lost in the big bad city now would it?" she said with a hand on her hip.

"We're fine Stacey, there's really no need for you to come with us," I said, stressing the point.

"Suit yourself, don't blame me when you're lost later on," she said with a shrug before heading back inside.

"I do appreciate your concern," I said, but she had already gone back inside.

"She seem a bit insistent to you?" Drake asked as we started walking south on Madison Ave.

"Ayep," I replied. "Someone doesn't like the idea of us nosing around."

"All the more reason for us to do it I'd say," Drake said.

We started walking and instantly noticed that there seemed to be no one living in close proximity to where we were stationed at the medical center, at least no one that we could find. We were about four blocks away before we saw the first sets of eyes peeking out from behind grime covered windows. We called out locations to each other as we spotted them. As we wandered, we tried to give off a casual air. To give off a stiff and defensive posture wouldn't make us any friends. We were both well armed, but except for our rifles, most of it was concealed.

A couple blocks down, and we saw a small group of people gathered in front of a building. When we got closer, we figured it had to be one of the stores that Stacey mentioned. If we were going to find people to interact with, this would probably be the place. The people in front of the store noticed us quickly and stared as we got closer. You could see their demeanor change the closer we got. The mistrust was almost tangible. We were outsiders and they knew it instantly. I saw Drake smile and give an older woman a nod as we passed her. In return she looked at him as if he were a ghost.

I gave a hearty and happy "Hello," to two guys I saw sitting on the curb, waiting for their turn in line. They looked to be in the thirties. One was wearing a ratty looking blue Carhart work coat, faded blue jeans with holes in the knees, some filthy looking Nike's and a tattered Yankees cap. The second was almost identical except he had an olive drab army jacket. They both had full beards and looked as if it had been awhile since they had bathed. Glancing around, the rest of the people looked very similar, with ragged dirty clothes. One of them scowled at me, while the other flipped me the bird. "Well, with such a great New York welcome, how could we not stop for a bit to chat?" I asked sarcastically.

"You'd think we were wearing Red Sox jerseys," Drake said. I distinctly heard someone mutter "Fuck you," in our general direction.

"Maybe if we try inside," I said, heading for the door of the market. The two men stood and quickly blocked my way, "Get in line like everyone else," the taller one said.

"We're not buying anything, we're just here to look around is all," I said as I tried to step around them.

"I don't care what you're doin' I said get in line," The taller man said again, sliding his hand into his jacket. Drake had his pistol out and pointed at the man before he even finished getting his hand IN his jacket. "You're gonna wanna slide that hand out slowly," Drake said, motioning to him.

The man wasn't stupid or suicidal, so he did as he was told. "Listen, we really do just wanna look around and maybe talk to some folks. We aren't here for trouble, actually we're here to help you," I said, trying to defuse the situation.

"You can look around all you like, but you ain't gonna find anyone that'll talk to you," The shorter of the two said.

"And why is that?" I asked.

He stalled for a second before saying, "Cuz no one knows you,"

"Hmm, is that the only reason?" I asked him.

"Well, that and you're from Boston. That'd be another good reason," he said with a smirk.

"We don't want any trouble either," The tall one started. "We're just here to pick up a little food, not make new friends."

"I guess we'll just be moving along then," I said as I glanced over at Drake who nodded in return.

"Pleasure meeting you all," Drake said as we continued south on Madison Ave.

"You know you'd probably be better off just goin back to the hospital," the taller man said as we left. I just gave him a wave as we continued on.

"Okay, so they REALLY don't want us wandering around," Drake said.

"Yeah, now I just wanna figure out why," I said.

"Or, we could just go back to the hospital. I mean do we really need to know?" Drake asked.

"Did you really believe that I was going to think that was a good idea?" I asked Drake.

"Of course not, it's far too logical an idea for you to even entertain," he answered.

We did see some more of the blocked off streets, a couple with armed men. I still wasn't sure why some were guarded and others weren't. The men standing behind the cars saw us, but took little to no notice of us. It was a few blocks further down before we ran into anymore people. They saw us coming and scurried into the buildings. I could hear the bolts locking as we went by. There was a couple walking diagonally across the street. They were heading toward one of the buildings as I spoke up, hoping to get their attention. "Hello there!" I said. They continued walking, not even flinching when they heard me. "I said hello there." They were an older couple. He was a bit hunched, while she kind of shuffled along. She had a hooded sweatshirt that, at one point, was red. He wore a long wool jacket and black gloves.

"I think maybe they don't wanna talk to us Mack," Drake said.

"I'm thinking at this point that I don't fucking care," I answered, "Hey, you wanna hold up a second?" I said, speeding up.

"Mack, calm down a bit," Drake said.

"I SAID HOLD UP!" I yelled, grabbing the man by the shoulder and spinning him around. The woman screamed and I saw terror in the man's eye. He was on the verge of tears.

"Please leave my husband alone," the woman said, pleading.

"I just wanted to talk to you two for a minute is all, I'm not trying to hurt you," I said, feeling confused.

"Well if you don't wanna hurt us, you should just let us go home then," she said quietly.

"Shut up Amy!" the man said suddenly angry.

"What's that supposed to mean?" I asked her.

"Nothing, we need to go," she said as she turned and quickly walked away. Her husband glowered at her and then ran off to catch her.

I stood there scratching my head as Drake came up next to me. "So, it seems that someone doesn't want us wandering around, OR talking to anybody," he said.

"Yeah, all of this is very weird," I replied.

"I bet we could find a bunch of answers down at Grand Central," he said.

"You may very well be right my friend. It's a good thing we're heading down that way," I said as we started walking south again.

It took us another half hour, or so, to get into the area of Grand Central Station. We had seen numerous other people and they all avoided us like the plague. I had tried to say "hi," to a couple more on our way down there, but I soon gave up. They wouldn't even make eye contact with us as we passed by them. I was noticing as we walked, that there weren't a lot of buildings that had toppled in this area. There were a few that were definitely not as stable as I would have liked, but unlike Boston, it seemed that most streets weren't blocked by falling rubble, at least not in this area.

We came to the street that would lead us to the terminal when I motioned for Drake to keep walking down Madison Ave. He raised an eyebrow at me, but kept walking. "I thought it might be a good idea to come up on it quietly. I don't necessarily want to go in yet, but I do wanna get a look at it," I said as we turned left a block later to come around the front side of the station.

"Yeah, it might piss our host off a bit if we just barged in. Especially, if he's hiding something," Drake agreed.

"Exactly, I'd like to wait until after we get rid of the troops before I piss off Riley. That is, if I even have to piss him off at all," I said, peeking around the corner to get my first glimpse.

"Oh, I'm sure you'll find a reason to piss him off," Drake said, chuckling.

"I usually do," I said. It was huge. I was looking at the front façade of Grand Central Station from a block away and it was still huge. I had never spent a lot of time in New York back before the Storm. Being from Boston, it was kinda frowned upon. We didn't actually hate each other. We just had different philosophies on what made a great city. Granted, most of us did indeed hate the Yankees. Then again, I guess most people did.

There was an elevated section of road that looked like it led to a drop off point. Part of that road had caved in at some point during the last five years. Otherwise, it was intact and somewhat well maintained. There were armed patrols outside. It looked like there were at least two men with rifles by the doors, with at least one wandering patrol. I was guessing that Riley was paranoid enough to have men stationed at the corners of the massive building as well.

Drake and I walked across the open street and under the elevated section of road. Drake kept going and stood on the far side of the overpass. We were both keeping to the shadows and somewhat hidden by the pillars holding up the road. We were counting guards and patrols, as well as how frequently they walked their route. I knew we couldn't stay here looking guilty for long, but a quick glimpse might be helpful. After about ten minutes, I walked casually over to where Drake was and we both continued to the far side of the street. Looking down the long empty street, leading back the way we had come, I could barely make out one of the car barricades a half a mile away.

There was a shell of a stripped down mustang. I slid up on the hood, reached into my jacket and pulled out the cigarette case that Riley had given me the night before. I popped it open and flipped open the cover of my Zippo. Flicking my thumb along the wheel, I lit the metal lighter. I stared at the cigarette for a few moments, pondering what we had seen. I put one end in my mouth and held the Zippo at the other. Taking a long drag, I held it in for a short time before letting out a big breath. I could almost feel the nicotine seeping into my bloodstream.

## Chapter 8

I sat on the hood of the Mustang, watching my cigarette burn away. I was trying to figure out my next move. I took a drag and flicked the ashes. I could feel Drake's eyes on me long before I glanced over at him. "What now?" he asked.

"Now, we go see Mr. Riley," I said, with a nod to myself as I slid off the hood and flicked the cigarette away.

"I thought we were just down here to take a look at the OUTSIDE," he said as we walked down to the end of the block.

"We were, and we did. Now it's time to see the inside," I said. We walked up onto the street that would take us to the overpass and right to the front door.

"Not that I'm usually one for prudence, but is this, a good idea?" he asked, walking next to me.

"Probably not," I said, "But when has that ever stopped me?"

"Well I'd say it was pretty obvious from the folks we ran into on the way down here, that Riley would like us to stay put," Drake argued.

"Yep, which is exactly why I'm here now, I just wanna peek. I won't snoop too much," I said. The area around Grand Central seemed to be deserted, even though I could feel dozens of eyes on me. It looked to me like Riley had the couple blocks around the station cleared out and was stationing his men in the surrounding buildings. Made sense, it's what I would've done.

As we got closer, I saw the guards out front take notice of us. Two of them began walking toward us. I stopped about a hundred feet from the door and let them come to us. "You got a reason for bein' here?" the one on the right asked.

"We were just in the neighborhood and thought we'd stop by to see Mr. Riley. Y'know, to thank him for the wonderful hospitality he's shown us," I said with a smile.

"Oh, they're from the hospital," the other guard said.

"Let me call in and see what they say," the first guard said to me.

"Sure, take your time," I said, leaning against the guard rail.

He stepped away from prying ears and called in on an old walkie-talkie radio. It took him a full minute, at least, to start back toward us.

69

"Okay, come with us, they said the boss will meet you in the lobby," he said, waving us forward as he turned and made his way back to the doors.

The glass doors now had steel plates welded behind them for added security. Once I got inside, it almost took my breath away. I'm sure that it looked much better before the storm, but even now, I was still impressed. The place was gigantic and the stone work was gorgeous. I'd bet they had made some changes, but I couldn't tell what they were. Most of the over head lights still seemed to be working and it was bright.

In stark contrast to the bright light and stone work beauty of the station were the people that we saw off in the corners. At the top of the stairs I caught a glimpse of a couple ducking down a side corridor. One of them had dropped something. She had tried to come back and get it, only to be grabbed and pulled down the hall by the guy she was with. I could clearly tell that it had been a syringe that she had tried to pick up. Tucked away on the main floor behind the stairs was a heavily bearded man who was curled up on a bench drooling on himself. I'd have thought he was just sleeping, if I hadn't noticed the big bottle of Jack Daniels tucked under his head, being used as a pillow.

At the far end of the station I could see two bodies entangled in each other. It looked as if they were getting very friendly on one of the wooden benches. I wasn't exactly positive what was going on, since it was so far away, but I could see that the girl who looked to be on her back was strawberry blond and wearing a pirate hat. Her male friend looked as if he could be Asian. "Is he wearing a spiked German army helmet?" I asked Drake as we walked slowly toward the stairs.

"Seriously, that's what you're curious about?" he mumbled softly.

"Why, what are you looking at?" I asked.

"I'm trying to figure out if her finger is… where I think it is," he answered, squinting off into the distance.

I blinked a couple times and took a second look, "Hmm, yep I'm gonna have to say that it most definitely is, and he doesn't seem to mind," I said with a small shudder.

"Daaaamn," was all Drake had to offer.

"Shhh, here he comes," I said, nudging Drake in the ribs.

Riley stood on the landing at the bottom of the first short flight of stairs. "Hello Mack, and welcome to my humble abode!" he exclaimed with his arms open wide.

"Pretty fancy digs ya got here," I said as I shook his hand and looked around the lobby. For the most part, it was a large open area that had hallways leading off in opposite directions. I couldn't see down them, so I had no idea how long they were.

"It's alright, I got it real cheap when the previous owners took off," he said, chuckling.

He led us down the next flight and over to the right where there was a space set up for relaxing. Someone had put down a plush rug and had moved in a bunch of comfy looking furniture. He motioned for us to have a seat. "Can I get you boys a drink?" he asked as he sat in a large, soft looking seat.

"Sure, beers good," Drake said, taking a seat himself.

Riley gave him a nod and spoke to the man standing next to his chair. He in turn walked off, more than likely, to get our beer.

"Was there something I can do for you boys?" Riley asked.

"Not really, I just thought it might be nice to come down and thank you for all the incredible hospitality," I said cordially.

"No need to thank me at all Mack, glad to do it, if it gets the army out of our hair," he said. One of his guards came over and whispered in his ear. He thought for a moment and then smiled at us before excusing himself. "Be back in a second," he said as he walked off and down the left hand corridor.

A minute later, a petite girl brought us two ice cold beers. She popped the tops and handed them to us without making eye contact. She'd have been pretty, if not for the huge scar running diagonally down her right cheek. "Thank you…" I said, pausing for her to tell me her name.

"Andrea," she said.

"Thank you Andrea, nice to meet you, I'm Mack," I said.

"You're the people from Boston right?" she said, looking around like she had done something wrong.

"Yeah, we're here to help out," I said, before taking a sip of my beer.

"Are you really here to help?" she asked quickly.

"Yeah, of course, why?" I asked, raising an eyebrow.

"Never mind," she said, looking nervous, "it was nice to meet you," she said as she spun and walked quickly away.

"That was weird," Drake said, looking at the brown bottle lovingly.

"No weirder than anything else we've seen today," I said.

"Touche," he said.

Riley returned quickly with Jimmy in tow, "Gentlemen, I'm afraid I'm going to have to cut our visit short. Jimmy here, will gladly take you back to the hospital," he said, sounding rushed.

"Is something wrong?" I asked as we stood.

"No no, nothing to be concerned about, just some internal matters that need my attention is all," Riley said with that huge shark like grin.

"We can find our way back, we're okay without Jimmy," Drake said, finishing off his beer.

"No, I insist. This way I'll know you're safe and it'll just be one less thing I have to worry about," he said, sounding more stern than I'd bet he wanted to.

"Sure, if it'll ease your mind, we'd be happy to take the ride," I said, blowing it off.

"Excellent, I'll be up to see you soon then," he said before he spun and walked quickly down the hall he had come from.

Jimmy gave a nod and a weak creepy kind of smile. He led us out a side door to the Caddy that Riley drove around in. He even held the back door open for Drake. Within a few minutes, we were getting out of it in front of the hospital. We thanked him for the ride, but he had driven off almost before I had closed the passenger door. It was pretty obvious that Jimmy was in a hurry as well. He, more than likely, didn't like being this far away from his boss. We waited for the Caddy to be out of site before we went inside.

I went straight to the office space where we had set up our command and control center. Gomez was there, as I had hoped, "Where's George?" I asked.

"Where did you expect him to be?" was the response I got from Gomez.

"Cafeteria?" I answered.

"Bingo," he said.

"Thanks," I said as I turned and walked down the hallway until I came to the open wooden doors that led into the Cafeteria. George was over in the corner by himself with a plate of something and a mug of coffee. He was looking through a manila folder as we walked up to him and grabbed a seat. "Hello boys," he said, peering over the tops of his taped together glasses.

"What ya got here?" Drake asked, picking at his plate.

"Some kind of meat and gravy, with what looks like real mashed potatoes," George answered with a shrug.

"Any clue what kind of meat?" I asked.

"Nope, and I don't care. This gravy is so good it could be chopped rat," he said, smiling.

"He's right, it's pretty damn amazing," Drake said, nodding to himself as he dipped his finger back into the brown sauce for another taste.

"Is there something you wanted, or were you really that curious about my lunch?" George asked, slapping at Drake's hand.

"We just went to visit Mr. Riley at Grand Central," I said softly.

"You did what?" George said, a bit louder than I'd have liked.

"I'm just here to diddle your gravy," Drake whispered from George's other side.

"Shut up," he said to Drake before turning back to me, "How'd it go?" he asked, dipping a piece of fresh bread into the gravy.

"It was interesting. No one would really talk to us and he rushed us out saying he had some other stuff to attend to. Something didn't seem right though," I said, scratching at my scruff.

"You sure you aren't just being paranoid? I mean, we spent years not talking to outsiders and don't you always have to attend to one thing or another," George reasoned.

"Yes, on both counts. It's just the way the locals were acting," I said, trying to plead my case.

"Let me guess, like they were afraid of you? I suppose that could be because they have no idea who you are, and you're carrying an AK-47," he said, looking at me like I was stupid.

"This was different. It was like they were afraid of him more than us," I said.

"I have no idea why. Hell I'd love to have this kind of food and luxury back home," he said.

"Yeah, your days are filled with Buffy and Twinkies, it must be tough," Drake said, snickering.

"It is, I'd much rather have Ding Dongs," George said.

"I'm serious here," I said, getting annoyed.

"I know you are," George said before turning to Drake, "Is he just being paranoid?"

"It'd be so much fun to say yes and watch his head explode, but no, I don't think he is. Something weird is going on, but I'll be damned if I know what it is yet," Drake said.

"But they have it so easy here," George said with a sigh.

"Yeah that's the thing, the people that were so afraid to talk to us, they didn't look like they had it all that good," I said.

"Add that to the things that they tried to hide at Grand Central as well," Drake added.

"What were they hiding there?" George asked, looking back and forth at us.

"They tried to make us think it was all on the up, but they didn't do such a great job. I'm betting it's a bit more of a den of iniquity than they'd like us to believe," I said.

"Fuck, real coffee and whores? Sign me up. Why put up the front though?" George asked.

"I dunno yet," I replied.

"You know, everyone else is very happy the way things are going here," he said to me in all seriousness.

"I know," I said.

"You may actually break someone's heart if you're right and it may be mine," he said sighing.

I left George and Drake in the cafeteria to go find Brett, Hags and the other clan heads. George told me they were in one of the conference rooms planning out the strategy for the upcoming attack on the military. He told me he'd join me after he finished slurping down as much of the gravy as he could get a hold of. I found Chris out in the lobby, she spotted me and came skipping merrily toward me, "There's my man," she said as she wrapped her arms around my shoulders and gave me a big kiss.

"Skipping, really?" I asked.

"Why wouldn't I be skipping? I had scrambled eggs and cinnamon toast for breakfast this morning. Real eggs! Do you have any idea how long it's been since I've had real eggs?" she asked

"Well considering what you just said, I'd have to guess since breakfast," I said, grinning.

"I mean before that!" she said, poking me in the chest.

"Ah, before this morning, yeah, it would have been awhile," I agreed.

"I have working equipment, and none of my patients are in danger of dying… at the moment," she said, "So yeah, I'm happy enough to skip all the way home."

"Good, I'm glad your end of things are going well hon," I said with a small smile.

"Why, what's wrong on your side of things?" she asked, looking concerned.

"Nothing, yet," I said.

"Ah, so you're being paranoid. I'd like to tell you to relax and enjoy, but I've been married to you long enough to know that's not gonna happen." She leaned in and gave me a short kiss, "I can't stop you from worrying, but at least try and enjoy some of this. You, more than most, deserve a break now and again."

"You're very cute," I said pulling, her close and kissing the top of her head, "I'll come find you later for dinner or something."

"Ooo, or something sounds nice. I mean, we do have our own room for the first time in months," she said, grinning evilly.

"Since when do we need a room?" I asked.

"True," she said, giggling. She turned and sauntered off knowing I was watching. "See you later hon, love you," she said over her shoulder before disappearing around a corner.

I turned to continue on my way to the conference room when I heard Anne calling to me from somewhere above me. I scanned around and found her coming down the stairway behind me. Walking over to the railing I leaned against it, waiting for her to come down. "What's up?" I asked.

"Hi," she said as she gave me a quick hug, I was looking for you earlier."

"Yeah, me and Drake went for a walk," I explained.

"Anything interesting?" she asked.

I shook my head and asked, "What did you need me for?"

"Well, first thing was to tell you how awesome this place is. I feel spoiled here. It's like a spa resort compared to home," she said.

"I keep hearing that," I said.

"Secondly, I was wondering how long we were gonna be here?" she asked.

"Not sure yet, why?" I replied.

"Well, Sam is getting kind of close to delivery. We were kinda hoping to not be on the road when she does," she said.

"Oof, That I have no idea of yet, but I will keep it in mind and get back to you," I said. I turned once again to leave and yet again heard, "Hey Mack," from behind me.

"Jesus Christ! What?" I said, spinning to find a smirking Drake.

"A little annoyed?" he asked.

"A little, what do YOU want?" I asked.

"Nothing, I expected you to be in the conference room by now. I got bored picking at George's plate, so I figured I'd join you," he said, shrugging.

"Good, let's go, before someone else distracts me," I said, walking quickly to get out of the lobby. "Hey, did you know Sam is almost due?"

"Due for what?" he asked, looking confused.

"To have the baby," I answered, glancing over at him as we walked.

"Oh that! She is huh? I just figured I'd wake up one day and there'd be a three year old looking all cute, waiting for his first skating lesson," he said.

"Wow, you're gonna be a great dad," I said, chuckling.

"I'm gonna teach him how to skate. What more am I supposed to do?" he asked, grinning.

"It is a necessary skill I suppose," I said, turning to the wooden door leading to the conference room.

"Yeah, I mean I'm gonna wait until he's at least four before I start stick and puck control, sheesh," he said, walking into the room.

"Aww see, you really do care," I said, shaking my head.

"What're you two going on about?" Art asked, sipping on a mug of coffee.

"Stick control," Drake said.

"Should two guys really be talking about that in public?" he asked totally deadpan.

"Wow, everyone's funny today," I said with a sigh.

"Some of us are always funny," Art replied.

"How are things going here?" I asked, rolling my eyes.

"Swimmingly," Brett answered.

"We've been putting together the plans for the attack. I'm glad the general could spare a few minutes to take a peek at them," Hags said sarcastically.

I meant to be here bright and early. We ended up taking a walk and got distracted," I said, looking down at the map they had sprawled out on the long table.

"A walk?" Art asked.

"Yeah, we went up to Grand Central," I answered.

"To do what?" Art asked, eyeing me with suspicion.

"To check it out, and to thank Riley for the hospitality," I said, shrugging.

"Uh huh," was all Art said.

"Well, that was very nice of you," Brett said.

"I thought so," I agreed.

"You were casing the joint," Hags said.

"Yep," I again agreed.

"That was very nice of you," he said, smirking.

"Again, I thought so," I grinned.

"Huh?" Brett asked.

"Nevermind," Hags said.

Art laughed and asked," Did you discover anything interesting?" he asked.

"Nothing that I can put a finger on yet," I said.

"You think something is up?" Art asked.

"Dunno yet, I hope I'm just being paranoid," I answered.

"Paranoia isn't always a bad thing," Hags said, leaning back in his chair.

"Amen to that, brotha," Drake said.

We spent the next couple of hours going over the locations of the troops and how we were going to split up our men for the attack. Stacey had provided us with detailed information about location and equipment. We figured we had enough men by ourselves to push the military out of here for good, so we went ahead with our planning. We knew that Riley would be by later on, but I was pretty sure he would be happier if we already had a plan in place that we could just plug his men into. He didn't seem like all that much of a strategist to me, at least not a military strategist.

A little later, I left the conference room and made my rounds. I checked in with Gomez and George in the Command Center. They filled me in on our communications set up. It seems they had run an antenna up to the roof of the building and that we should be able to talk to each other with the radios at almost all of the attack points. They had sent a couple men out to test the range.

From there, I had Drake round up the team leaders to go over the particulars of the plan. It took us longer to gather everyone up than it did for the meeting itself. We had all done this numerous times at this point and everyone knew their roles. After going over the particulars, they headed off in different directions to gather their teams and fill them in.

Drake and I found the rest of Alpha and had the same meeting as the rest of the team leaders. It would be my first mission with the three new members and I was anxious to see how they'd do. From everything Drake and Tom told me they were all very good. I was just happy to be able to get to see it for myself. We were going to be in charge of the southernmost section of the city. Mark's team would be with us along with a few hundred men.

Once that wrapped up, I made my way down to the infirmary to check on Chris. She and Eva were working away. I curled up on a couch with Lily, enjoying the peace and quiet for a bit. There weren't a lot of wounded left for Chris to take care of at this point, so she was keeping her and Eva busy by doing an inventory of all the supplies and meds.

Sure enough, when Riley showed up a few hours later, he was seemingly stunned at our simple plan and essentially, gave us control over his men. He told us that he would station them wherever we needed him to. He assured us, repeatedly, that they would be ready to go and fight to the last man if necessary. After the short meeting was over, he decided to join us for dinner.

After dinner, he had whipped out another bottle of Johnny Walker Blue and we all sat around having a couple drinks. The first time we had done this, it seemed as if he had been trying to impress us. This time was a bit different. His focus seemed to be much more centered on Eva. Before finishing my first drink I had noticed it. I had caught a few uncomfortable glances from the others before I had poured my second. Conversation broke off into smaller groups and Riley seemed to take Eva off into a corner, even though they never left the couch. Teddy looked to me a few times silently asking me if he should run interference, and every time I shook him off. Eva didn't seem to mind the attention at all and I was very curious to see how it all played out. She'd let me know if she needed any help.

The evening wore on and people trailed off. George and Teddy were still hanging on and Riley was still working hard on Eva while Jimmy loomed off in a corner. He had finally taken a seat, but it was well away from the rest of us. "I suppose it's getting late," Riley said, looking crushed.

"We do have a big day coming up," I said.

"Yeah we do," he said. "God, it'll be nice to be free again."

"I was wondering, would you like to come back with me and see Grand Central Station?" he asked Eva. She paused for a moment and peeked around him to me. I gave a nearly imperceptible shake of my head, her eyes quickly returned to Riley's.

"I really shouldn't. I'd love to, but we should probably wait until after," she said seeming, to be truly sorry.

"Yeah, that makes sense actually, not like you're going anywhere," he said, and suddenly I saw that tiny flash of anger. It was only for a split second. Man, did he hate being told no.

He spun and smiled at the rest of us before saying a brief goodnight. As he and Jimmy walked toward the other end of the lobby, Riley held up the mostly empty bottle over his head and went on to declare victory in the coming battle for freedom liberty and the love of a fine cheese.

"I think I should be calling it a night as well," George said as he staggered off, giving a wave over his shoulder.

I could see that Teddy was looking tense and I think both Eva and I knew why. "Teddy, could you give Eva and I a few minutes?" I asked my old friend.

"'course, I should head to bed as well. Need to get an early start, still a lot to get done," he said before he walked off.

"Y'know," Eva said as she got up and walked over to me on the couch, "I had no intention of going." she flopped down on the cushion next to me, laid her head on my lap and propped her feet up on the arm. "I figured. You were never stupid, somewhat impulsive maybe, but not stupid," I said as I ran my hands through her wavy brown hair.

"I was checking with you to see if you WANTED me to go," she said.

I chuckled, taken somewhat by surprise. "Why would I want you to go?" I asked, looking down into her deep green eyes.

"I figured you might need me to spy a bit," she giggled.

"Ahh, well thank you for the offer, but I'd rather you stay safe," I said, shaking my head.

"I'm here to help," she said, smiling up at me.

"You already do plenty. Besides, you wanna help, smile at Teddy a bit tomorrow, so he can relax a little," I said.

"Teddy is funny," she closed her eyes and grinned.

I draped my arm across the front of her shoulders. "What's going on there?" I asked conversationally.

"Nothing yet, I mean, he's nice enough," she said as I felt her shrug, " I suppose I should figure it out, one way or the other. I should probably be popping out some kidlets in the near future, for the good of the species."

"You've always been so wonderfully logical," I said, grinning to myself.

"You love me for my brain huh?" she said, poking me in the side.

"That and your sparkling personality," I said, tapping her on the tip of her button nose. I noticed the tiny line of freckles across the bridge of it and smiled to myself.

"Riiight," she said, smirking.

"Hey, I've always loved you like a little sister," I said.

"Yes, but who's little sister?" she asked.

"HEY!" I said, tickling her ribs. She squealed and squirmed trying to get away. Pushing herself almost entirely off the couch. She popped up onto her knees and leaned heavily on my shoulder, her head pressed against my neck.

"Do you know how big a crush I used to have on you, back in the day?" she asked, breathing softly in my ear.

"Oh? Funny, you may have wanted to mention that back then," I said, glancing at her out of the corner of my eye.

"Nah, the age gap always made me nervous, I figured you'd just laugh at the silly girl, but yeah, it was… pretty ginormous," she said, giving me a soft peck on the cheek before leaning back with her legs folded up beneath her.

"I won't say that the thought didn't cross my mind," I said honestly.

"Oh, I know it did," she said, smiling evilly, "crossed mine too, a lot."

"Uh huh," I replied.

She stood and sighed heavily, "I shoulda just banged you when I had the chance, instead I wussed out after a kiss. Ah well, maybe someday Chris will decide you two should have a threesome and I'll get my chance." She leaned in, stared deeply into my eyes and brushed her full, soft lips against mine for the briefest of instants. "I'm gonna head off to bed hon."

"G'night," was all I could manage.

"Oh, thank you, for always being a gentleman back then. I've always loved you for that. Well, that and for always watching out for me," she said, reverting back to little sister mode, as she gave me a quick hug before turning and walking off.

"Fuckin' tease," I said, shaking my head and chuckling to myself.

After a few minutes of calm and quiet, I pushed myself up off the couch, wincing as my knees cracked when I stood. I shoved my balled up fists into the small of my back and stretched out my beat up old muscles. Making my way down to our room, I opened the door quietly to find Chris sound asleep and Lily curled up in the little spoon position. She had looked up as I came in and quickly drifted back off to sleep. I tried to slip into bed without disturbing Chris, but she stirred and rolled over. Lily shifted position slightly, snuffled me with her cold nose and then rested her chin on my thigh. I scratched her behind the ears until she fell back to sleep. I started to doze off shortly, smiling at thoughts of a past long gone.

## Chapter 9

The next day had been filled with planning, handing out equipment as well as making sure that everyone and everything was in order for the attack. By the time the sun came up on the morning of the attack all of my men were out in front of the hospital and ready for action. Granted, we were still waiting for Riley and his contingent to show up, but my troops were cocked, locked and ready to rock.

Riley showed up a half hour or so later. We went over the plan again with him and his officers, if you wanted to call them officers. His troops were more like a resistance force than an army. Then again, that is exactly what they were. They seemed to be well enough trained for what we were about to do though, so I couldn't complain too much. If all went well, this would be pretty simple and we could be back by sun down. Within the hour, Riley's troops were set up and ready to go.

The idea was for us to split into four groups, so that we could hit all the different sites at the same time. The military didn't have enough men to hold New York after Riley had pushed them back, but they did have enough to block off every road going in or out of the city. My team was going to hit the camp furthest south, so we left first. Our target was much further out than the other three. They were going to be within a couple miles of each other the whole attack. We had to get all the way down to the other end of Brooklyn before we got to our target. The other three teams walked to their targets, with only the commanders having vehicles. We, on the other hand, stuffed as many into the trucks and vans as we could because of the distance. Our troops would have been far too tired to fight if we made them walk. That and we'd have had to wait another day just for us to get there.

There were two hundred and fifty of our men and one hundred of Riley's. Once we got to the area, his men would lead ours into position. The military had taken up positions in natural choke points, so we would eventually have to drive straight at them. The idea was to get close enough BEFORE doing that to make their cannons ineffective. According to Riley's numbers, we should have them out numbered almost three to one. The hope being, that they would break and run causing a rout. That way, we'd only have a small mop up to do and there wouldn't be a large loss of life on either side.

The military now, is not nearly what it was, back before the storm. Most of their troops now enlisted to have some kind of food or shelter for them or their families. I found that they tend to run long before a real soldier would. Granted, not all of them are this poorly trained, just most of them. A lot of the well trained soldiers never made it through the storm. Finding new troops when everyone left in your country is either starving or freezing is easy if you have food and heat. The problem the military had is that most of their good officers died as well. Soldiers are only as good as the people who train them. Most of these new recruits were not trained by the elite soldiers that were the US military.

It took us almost an hour to get into position. Once we were set, I gave George a call, "Baby bear to Papa bear, we are ready to go."

"'Bout time Baby bear, everyone else has been green light for twenty minutes," he answered.

"Good to know, I will call the ball momentarily," I said. "Copy that," was all George answered. I used the ear bud to check with the rest of Alpha as well as checked in with Riley, on a different radio to make sure, for the third time that we were all set and ready to go. He gave me a testy sounding affirmative. I took a deep breath and held the radio up to my mouth. I let it out before keying the microphone, "All units, green light," it was a simple sentence, but it was the "Go" sign we assigned for this mission.

"All units are a go Baby bear," I heard George confirm as he listened in on the unit specific channels back at the hospital with Gomez and his team. It was almost drowned out by the sound of engines and the roar of men charging into battle. We had men driving heavy vehicles as far up as they could to provide cover for our men instead of just charging into a choke point. They may not be the best of the best that the US military used to be, but I didn't think we needed to give them fish in a barrel to shoot at.

There was a commotion and I heard the rattle of assault rifles begin. Alpha and I were up on a small hill off to the side of the road. The rest of the team provided security for Drake and I as we communicated with the men forty yards away or so. Riley and his man Jimmy were standing nearby as well. He had decided to let me run the mission end of things, he just wanted to see the end of the military's occupation of HIS city.

I give the troops credit. They didn't break during the first wave of attack. Instead, they tried to turn their cannons around to face our onslaught. Unfortunately, too many of them had to stop firing in order to do it. They were quickly mowed down. A couple of Riley's men then tossed grenades under the cannon and it leapt half a foot of the ground as they exploded. I heard him curse and glanced over at him for a brief second. "Wasn't expecting it to be that loud," he said, shrugging.

"Just be glad they haven't fired the cannons yet," Drake said, staring into his binoculars. "Mack, send up the third team to the right side to flank the guys behind those sand bags over there."

"On it," I said before giving the orders through the ear buds. I quickly went back to watching my side of the action.

A couple minutes later, I heard George's voice coming from the radio, "Baby bear this is Papa bear, do you copy?"

"I copy Papa bear g'head," I mumbled.

"How goes it?" George asked.

"So far so good, they haven't broken off yet, but they've lost far more than we have," I answered.

"Outstanding sir, Three says it's just about to start wrapping things up. They're reporting large droves have dropped their weapons and run off at the outset," he reported.

"That'll cut down on our casualties," I said with a small grin.

"Woodsie, toss some cover fire for those men behind that car over there," Drake said, pointing. The chugging of the short barreled M-60 was thunderous right next to me. I could see the trail of his shots running from in front of the car Drake had pointed at to the sandbags where four soldiers had taken cover.

"Papa bear, I'll get back in touch when it quiets down here," I yelled. I heard a faint "Copy that," in my ear.

It seemed that Jim was feeling left out of the fun and started taking pot shots with his rifle as well. Things looked to be winding down and I noticed that there seemed to be less and less men behind the sandbags. Within a couple minutes, I saw the first raised hands as troops slowly stood up in surrender. I immediately called for a cease fire. The team leader, Mark, that had led the charge called for the troops to throw down all weapons and step out from behind the sandbags.

There was a roar from the troops as most of them raised their rifles in victory. The front twenty, covered what remained of the military. As for the rest of our men, some hooted, other hollered, fewer still fired off rounds into the air. "Hot damn that was nice!" I heard Eric exclaim from behind me.

"Gentlemen, excellent work indeed! You have my heartfelt gratitude for all of your assistance," Riley said, shaking my hand and giving me that shark like grin.

"Glad we could help you out sir," I said, clapping him on the shoulder. I could hear George in my ear telling me that team three was finally clear as well as two. Four was close, but not quite there yet. "Copy that, amazing work all around," I told him, "We are now clear as well."

"I'm going to head back and plan for the big victory celebration for us all tonight. You should get down there and join your men. I'm sure they'd want you with them," Riley said with his hand on my shoulder.

"Yeah, I believe you're right Riley. You should come too, your men are down there as well," I said, taking a few steps down the hill.

"No no, the party I'm gonna throw them, and you, tonight will more than make up for me not going down there. I'll see you in a bit for the festivities," he said as he turned and gave a wave as he and Jimmy walked over to his Caddy.

"All right boys let's go celebrate with the troops!" I said, walking slowly down the hill. I heard the door close and the Caddy drive off. George was telling me that four was clear as well now. I was thanking him for the great news when I heard the first shot. It started as one clear pistol shot ringing out. I spun to see where it came from and heard someone cry out. That was the last sound I heard before a deafening hailstorm of bullets erupted. From behind me I heard more shots, these were rifle rounds, and then I saw the dirt kick up near my feet. Everything was happening in slow motion. I saw from around the corner, a block behind us, men were flowing toward us. They weren't Army either. They were Riley's, men running at us full speed and firing. I heard screaming in my ear, as I ran back up the hill trying to find cover, **"MAAACK!"** I heard George's voice coming through the radio, **"FUCK MACK, IT'S A TRAP! THEY'VE TURNED ON ALL THE OTHER TEAMS!"**

I glanced down the hill as I dove over the ridge and saw that Riley's men had been the gunfire I heard. They had opened up on my men and were mowing them down. Most of my men were down, blood pooling around the bodies. Some were scrambling for cover where they could find it. The poor soldiers that had surrendered were long dead considering they were unarmed and between the two groups. They had just massacred all of them.

"Mack, what the fuck?" Drake asked as he flipped the selector on his AK-47 and fired at the group of at least fifty men that had appeared behind us.

**"FUCKIN' GODDAMN IT!"** I swore as I peeked over the ridge and fired a burst at the small detachment that had broken off. They're making their way toward us. **"WOODSIE, TOM, KEEP THESE FUCKERS HEAD'S DOWN!"** I screamed, pointing to the group coming up. **"JIM, ERIC, GET SOME COVER FIRE ON WHAT'S LEFT OF OUR MEN DOWN THERE!"** I said, pointing at the thirty or so men hiding behind cars and sandbags at the attack point. Drake and I joined Jim and Eric in trying to give our boys a fighting chance. We took out some of Riley's men, but they were well dug in. I watched in horror as five of Riley's men snaked their way through the sandbags and the rubble to one of the cannons. **"SOMEONE KILL THOSE FUCKS!"** I screamed as I unloaded a whole clip in their direction to no effect. They were too far off and I was too angry to be accurate. One of the others tagged one of them, but it was too late. In under a minute, they had the gun spun around. **"YOU NEED TO MOVE NOW!"** I screamed into the mic. Either my men didn't hear, or couldn't move. The cannon exploded and I felt it thunder in my chest. I watched as their position evaporate. **"NOOOOOOOOOOOOOO!"** I wailed.

**"JESUS CHRIST!"** Woodsie yelled behind me, "What the fuck was that?" he asked still holding off the men coming up the hill to murder us.

"They just killed them all," Drake said, barely above a whisper, staring at the smoking hole, that had been our friends.

"Mack, we need to go now. This ain't gonna get any better," Jim said, reloading his M-16.

"We're not going anywhere. We need to save whoever is left," I said, sitting there, staring blankly at Jim.

"Mack, he's right. There's no one left," Tom said, pulling me close and thunking his forehead against mine, tears streaming openly down his cheeks. "We gotta go."

**"LIL HELP HERE?"** Woodsie yelled over his shoulder. Eric and Jim were there, in a heartbeat, to help him tear up the few left that were coming up the hill.

"Oh Christ," I heard Drake say, "Okay, we're moving and now."

"What?" Tom asked glancing over his shoulder at him.

**"GO, NOW, EVERYONE!"** Drake yelled, grabbing me and Tom by the shirts and pulling us up as he tried to shove us in front of him, **"THEY'RE TURNING THE CANNON, MOVE!"** I glanced behind him and saw that the barrel of the big gun was swinging toward us. Obviously, someone had remembered we were here. We ran down the hill that Woodsie and Tom had just cleared. Bodies were strewn on the frozen ground now stained maroon with blood. I heard the cannon fire and felt the concussion push me forward as the spot where we had been moments earlier exploded. Chunks of dirt and rock rained down around us. Someone was screaming, but I was too focused on getting to the vehicles to care.

"Drake's on point. Get us the fuck out of here," I said as he ran by me.

"Copy that, goin' to the cars?" he asked.

"Yeah," I said, falling in behind Tom.

Across a street, through an old parking lot, and down a driveway we ran. I heard shouts behind us and shots being fired as we turned the corner onto the parkway. George was yammering over the radio and I flicked it off. The vehicles were less than twenty yards away. Woodsie spun, and emptied the last of the drum magazine to buy us a little time. Drake yanked the driver's door open and jumped inside the van. Tom hit the back door first, pulled it open, and I dove in as I heard Drake turn the engine over. I rushed forward as the others piled inside. Woodsie was the last in, sitting on the rear bumper he locked in a new drum and yelled for Drake to drive. Drake hit the gas and the van lurched. Woodsie would have tumbled out the back if not for Jim grabbing him by his harness and holding on. He muttered a "Thanks," and opened up. He paused only long enough to tell us that they had grabbed a couple cars as well.

I heard a bang and the van veered to the left, which actually, worked out well since we were turning that way. We took the turn too sharp and bounced as we went up over the curb. "What the hell?" Drake growled as he took a quick right.

"I think they got one of the back tires," I yelled over the machinegun fire.

"That's okay I took out one car and the other's pouring out some kind of fluid," Woodsie said over his shoulder while waiting for a target.

"Were running on rim, we need to lose these fuckers fast," Drake said as I finally got to climb into the passenger seat.

We took another quick left and right turn before I saw the spot. "Turn in here, quick," I said, pointing to a driveway to what looked like an old apartment building.

"We're clear for the moment, they can't see us," Tom called from behind us.

Drake slammed it in park, killed the engine and we got out as quietly as we could. He discovered that the left back tire had blown out. He kicked it hard as we set up a small security perimeter. I held up a hand for quiet and listened. I could hear the engine of the other vehicle. Because it had lost so much fluid it was rattling and making a chuffing sound as it was going to die soon. They had passed the street we had turned down and I heard the dying engine rattle off in the distance.

"We gotta get away from here. They will circle back," I said, checking my magazine.

"Can't we just change the tire?" Eric asked.

"We don't have time, Mack's right, we gotta go," Tom agreed.

"Drake's on point again. Go right out of here, stay off the main street. We'll find somewhere to hide a little later on," I said as Drake gave a nod and led us out. We crossed the street we were on, ducking down alleys and cutting through parking lots. We were being very careful every time we had to cross a street. I was hoping that Riley didn't have any men patrolling the area and so far, we had been lucky. After almost an hour of skulking our way back toward Manhattan, we found what looked to be an empty building. We watched it from a hiding spot across the street for at least ten minutes before we crossed two by two and darted inside.

It was an old school, from the looks of it. We secured the doors with an old rope that was hanging near the door. It took us a bit, but we swept the entire place and found it to be empty. Jim and Eric were guarding the front door, while Woodsie made sure the back doors were secure. Tom and Drake came with me to the top floor. I didn't know if being higher would help in this situation, but it couldn't hurt. I pulled out the radio and turned it on. I instantly heard Gomez repeating my call sign over and over. I keyed the mic and responded.

"JESUS, Mack, you scared the crap out of us. Hold one for Papa bear," Gomez said quickly.

"Copy that," I replied.

I waited about thirty seconds before I heard George, out of breath, on the other end, "What the fuck happened to you?"

"Sorry, we had to go dark for a little escape and evade. We're clearer now, but nowhere near safe," I answered.

"Mack, we need to talk," he paused. When he started again, he sounded on the verge of tears, "They're almost all dead Mack. He took out all of team three and I mean all, Buck, Jay, Ghana dead, all their men, dead. Team two got back first. It was Roy, his team and fifteen men, half of whom were severely wounded."

"We can do this when I get back George," I said, trying to stay calm.

"No we can't Mack, that's what I'm trying to explain," he said, sounding sad.

"Huh?" I asked.

"We may not be here by then. Team four, Teddy's team, managed to get a few of his men out, but they're all beat to shit as well. I've pulled in as much of our supplies as I could get a hold of, but I have no idea how long it'll last," he said.

"You brought in supplies? I asked, glancing at Drake who just shrugged.

"Yeah, I brought in the supplies. Shortly, after Teddy showed up, I rounded up some of the men left here to send an extraction team down to help you get out, after you went dark. I sent a hundred and fifty men out the front door of this fucking hospital and they didn't get thirty yards away before I watched them get FUCKING DECIMATED! Every one of them is dead Mack. He's laying siege to the hospital," George said.

I heard Tom curse and Drake just stared at the radio in disbelief. "Jesus," I whispered. "Make sure that place is buttoned up tight and get some snipers up top. Anyone comes within thirty feet of that place and you put a round through their fucking head," I said, trying to stay calm and figure shit out.

"You think I haven't done that already? Just get your asses back here, so we can go the fuck home," George said, sounding pissed.

"We're workin' on it. The problem is, they're hunting us at the moment and we don't have a car. It may take a while. Plus, I have some folks that need killing before we go home," I said.

"At this point, we've lost so many I just wanna get the rest of us out of here in one piece. How did we not see this?" George asked.

"I dunno, we're gonna head out soon. I think we may have lost our tail," I said before I saw Tom shaking his head slowly as he stared out the window. "Take care of everyone Papa bear. We'll be in touch soon."

I flipped off the radio and walked over to Tom, "What's up?" I asked.

"I've seen too many cars out there. They don't know we're here, but they're looking for us," Tom said.

"If we sit tight they should move on," I said.

"Unless they start going house to house instead, that's what I'd do if I left that big a loose end," Tom shrugged.

"Yeah, maybe they aren't as good at this as you are," I said, feeling tired.

"Ya think?" Tom said, exploding suddenly, "You really think they're not that good at this yet? **THEY FUCKING DESTROYED US! THEY DID, IN TEN MINUTES, WHAT THE FUCKING U.S. ARMY COULDN'T DO IN THREE YEARS, AND YOU THINK THEY'RE JUST GONNA LEAVE? WHEN DID YOU BECOME A FUCKING IDIOT?"** he was so close I could feel the spit hitting my cheek as he screamed. He was right. All I could do was sit there and take it.

I couldn't look one of my oldest friends in the face, so I stared at my boot tops and muttered, "I'm sorry, I screwed up." I felt his gloved hand around my throat before I finished the last word. With a roar he shoved and pinned me to the wall.

**"I DON'T WANT YOUR FUCKING APOLOGY! ALMOST ALL OUR FRIENDS ARE DEAD, DO YOU GET THAT YET?**

**JUST FUCKING FIX THIS, BEFORE WE ALL DIE!"** he bellowed before letting me go and slamming his fist into the wall next to my head.

"What exactly do you want me to do Tom? I didn't trust this prick from the beginning, but everyone loved all the cool stuff he kept giving us. I tried to tell people to be careful, and in the end I underestimated him as well We got **FUCKED, ROYALLY FUCKED!** Yeah, I get it Tom they're dead and we're screwed. You wanna give me a little bit to wrap my head around shit, so **MAYBE** I can pull a **FUCKING** rabbit out of my ass. Or would you just like me to snap my fingers and teleport us back to Boston?" I said, slamming my pointed finger into his chest, backing him almost all the way across the room.

"You're right, I'm sorry too," he said, after taking a minute to process it all.

"Good, now go around and get me an ammo and equipment count while I sit here and try to figure out how to get us at least back to the hospital," I said, sliding down in an empty corner of the room. I rubbed my tired eyes with my gloved fists.

"I'll just be over here if you need me," Drake said as he sat heavily on an old couch that had been left here. He dropped his rifle and let out a small groan as he rubbed his face and bowed his head.

After a few minutes, Tom returned with the numbers. They weren't encouraging at all. We had expected this to be a quick operation, so we neglected to bring any extra food, or a lot of ammo. We may have enough ammo, but how we were going to fight our way into the hospital if it's under siege when we get there is beyond me.

## Chapter 10

I stood off to the side of the window, staring out onto the streets below. I'm sure it looked like I was watching for patrols, and I was, to a degree. Mostly, I was thinking about all the men and close friends I'd just lost. They deserved to be brought home and buried with honor, but I'd more than likely never be able to do that now. The net that Riley's men had cast wasn't tight yet. If we gave them too much more time, it would be. Drake had cleared off a table and was staring at the map with Tom. They had been at it for over twenty minutes now and had tossed out at least three plans. Frustrated, Tom threw up his hands, "We need to get the hell out of here!" he said, coming toward me.

I nodded, still staring out the window. "Let's go then," I said.

"Isn't that what I'm working on a plan for?" Drake asked.

"Yeah, about that," I started, "You've both been at it for awhile, I don't think you're gonna find one," I said.

"So, how do you propose we get home then?" Drake asked, looking annoyed.

"We just go," I shrugged, still staring out the window.

"Oh, that sounds healthy," Tom said.

"Well, I'd ask if either of you has a better plan, but since I know you don't, I guess I won't bother," I said, turning to face two of my oldest friends. "We don't have time for this shit. Every minute we stay here, is a minute closer they get to either catching us or killing everyone we love. Let's just grab our gear and go. I know it doesn't sound great, but honestly, I'm hoping some of these fuckers do find us, just so I can kill some people. The amount of rage I have flowin' right this minute is immense. I myself, would rather put it to some use and hopefully, get us back to the hospital," I said, slinging my AK over my shoulder waiting for their response. There'd be time for grieving later.

"You know, as far as motivational, pick me up speeches go, it sucked," Tom said, smiling, "but he makes some good points. Let's get outta here."

"Okay, it's settled then, marching into the maw of certain death it is. I was hoping you'd suggest it at some point, took you long enough," Drake said with a wink.

The newer members of Alpha didn't like our plan as much as Tom or Drake, but they didn't complain when we laid it out for them. I checked in with George one last time and told him our location and that we were moving out. He gave us his usual "Happy hunting," and signed off. We were on our own, and he knew there was nothing he could do to help at the time. It annoyed him to no end to have as little control as he had right this moment. He must have been on the verge of pulling out what little hair he had left.

We left through the back of the building and down an alley next to an old church behind it. Tom made the sign of the cross and said a little prayer as we were passing by. Drake was on point and stopped at the corner of the church to check for other signs of life. He gave the signal and we all moved up. We crossed the small street and traveled up 82nd street. At 3rd we turned right and decided to go straight for a while. We were trying to make up time, as well as, put distance between us and the attack site. A straight line was the best way to do both. Thankfully, we hadn't seen anyone since we left the school. The area was so large and densely packed with buildings that we could get lucky and not run into anyone at all. I wasn't gonna put any money on that, but at this point anything was possible.

As we walked, we saw people in the upper windows of some of the buildings. From the looks on their faces they were civilians and not Riley's men. I was never happier that there were no more phones. I'm sure some of them would have turned us in, in a New York minute, if they thought they could get some of his fresh food. After we hit 67th street there was a park. We made our way into the copse of dead trees and found an outcropping of rocks to take cover behind as we took a break. The team set up a loose security while Drake and I checked the map. We were heading in the right direction and had been lucky so far, but we still had a long way to go.

We were coming up on route 278, in a perfect world, I'd have followed that to get back. It was far too open and we'd be too easily trapped if we went that way. Instead, I saw a huge park only a mile and a half or two away. It was getting to be mid afternoon and trying to stay undetected made for much slower traveling. If we could get there by sun down we could rest for a few hours. It would make for much faster traveling in the dark. If we ran across their patrols we could take them out quietly, and if they were traveling in a vehicle, we'd hear it as well as see the lights off in the distance. We quickly came to the conclusion that the dark would be our greatest advantage and hopefully our savior.

It did take us another three hours to travel the short couple of miles. We left the smaller park and cut through a large parking lot that led us to a group of smaller buildings. We could see Route 278 in front of us before we bolted for the protection of the overpass. We quickly ducked off the main street and headed down what was 64th street. We traveled down there until we got to 5th Ave. It was around dusk at this point and the light was fading fast. We ran parallel to the street, cutting through back alleys and climbing fences until it got fully dark. Then we picked up a bit of time by traveling down the middle of the Ave. We hooked a right and made our way over to 7th Ave. which, after a mile or so, brought us directly into the park. The place was huge and looked to be filled with plenty of places for us to hide out in. Once we were deep into the park, we picked a small utility building and ducked inside. It was barely big enough for the six of us, but it was the first time all day that we had felt safe. Cramped or not, it was better than being outside exposed to the elements, and Riley's men.

It was pitch black inside with the door closed. We sat for a few minutes just catching our breath and decompressing. There wasn't a lot of chatter at first. A couple minutes passed, I heard rustling as people started to wiggle out of their harnesses and packs. Someone reached up and pulled the door open for a bit of the fading light.

"Grab a drink and have some food, if you carry any on you, so we can get a few hours shut eye," I said, rummaging around in my pack to see if I had any of my jerky left. I loved jerky. I almost always had some with me in case of emergencies. At the moment though, I couldn't remember if I refilled my supply of the leathery goodness. I found a few pieces in a baggy in one of the side pockets of my pack. It wasn't a lot, but it'd have to do.

"I have to pee," Woodsie said, coming over to the door. I stood to make room for him to get by.

"You wanna take the 60 with you?" I asked.

"Oh, I suppose I don't need to. It might give us a bit more room in here if it was stowed in a corner huh?" he asked with a goofy grin.

"It might," I said, returning his smile.

I watched him struggle with taking his harness off. It had a security strap that helped him hold the 60 steady. I'm sure he was big enough to handle it without it, but why not use the tool that makes life easier? I pulled the door open and guided the bull in the china shop outside. He had tangled himself up in his harness and started spinning in circles as if this would help at all. I steadied him, grabbed the main clasp and popped it open for him. He grunted happily and smiled like an innocent little kid, "Thanks!" he said, shrugging out of the contraption. I grabbed the .60 from him as he undid another clasp holding it to his harness. I glanced down and saw the strap had something written on it. Woodsie had disappeared around the corner to do his business, while I flipped the strap over to see what was on it. I figured it was a brand name or something. I chuckled to myself and shook my head as I read it. Woodsie came back around the corner, "What?" he asked, raising an eyebrow at me.

"You named your gun heavy?" I asked.

"No," he said, quite seriously.

"Why does it say heavy on the strap then?" I asked, becoming very curious.

"Cuz it is heavy," he said, still completely deadpan.

"Not to nitpick, but you misspelled heavy, which is why I thought you had named it," I said, handing the 60 back to him.

"I did?" he asked, glancing down at the strap that said HEVY. I just nodded and smiled. "Hey, guess who has two thumbs and a learning disability?" he asked as he held the .60 between his knees.

"Who?" I asked, barely holding a straight face.

"This guy right here!" he exclaimed, hooking his thumbs toward his chest and wiggling them with yet another big innocent looking grin.

"Excellent, I'll have to remember that for the future," I said, chuckling as I headed back inside with the others.

"Sorry, I make jokes when I'm nervous, or in this case, scared shitless," he said, hanging his head a little.

"Its fine big guy, we're all scared," I said, putting a hand on his shoulder.

"You don't look it," he said, glancing over at Drake who had already curled up and fallen asleep.

"We've just been doing this a lot longer, trust me, it's not that we're not scared," I said, slumping down into the corner.

"That's good to hear because you can't probably see this, but I'm sitting here shaking cuz I'm so scared," Eric said from the opposite corner.

"Agreed," I heard Jim say.

I smiled softly to myself. "You all did great today, honestly. We'll be fine. You'll feel better when we're back with the others," I said, trying to sound optimistic.

"Yeah, Mack's right. You all did great considering this is your first real shit storm," Tom said, sounding half asleep as well, "I believe Drake here pissed himself the first time we were in a world of shit, back in the day."

"I believe you're correct sir," I said, agreeing with him. He hadn't, but if it made these poor guys feel better, he did.

"Well, at least I didn't do that," Eric said with a sniff. Thankfully, it was dark, so he could let the tears flow without feeling embarrassed.

"I think I may have shat myself a bit, but I'm not checking that until I have to," Jim said with a small chuckle.

I pulled out the radio and flipped it on. It only took a minute for George to respond to my calls. "What's the good word?" I asked, trying to sound hopeful.

"Grim would be a good word if I had to pick one," he replied.

"Lovely," I said with a sigh.

"I'm pretty sure we're surrounded, but we can't see anyone, and no one has come looking for our surrender," he said, sounding tired.

"He's probably gonna let you sweat it out a bit before he tries that, or he's too busy trying to find us. Either way, let's hope it buys us time enough to get back there," I said.

"What're we gonna do when you get back here?" George asked.

"Haven't gotten that far yet," I said, being honest.

"Awesome," he grumbled.

"We're hold up somewhere for now. We'll move out in a few hours when it's good and dark. We're hoping to be there by sun up, but no promises," I said.

"Hopefully, we'll still be around to greet you. Stay safe," he said.

"Copy that," I replied and shut the radio off.

It was about 9PM when we left the safety of the utility shed. It was an inky blackness as we walked across the park. Because of the cloud that hung constantly over us now there was no light from the moon and the stars. On a good night, you could see a hazy outline of the moon above you. Tonight, was not one of those nights. As much as I hated the idea, we had to use our flashlights to get us through the rocky and uneven territory of the park. Even then, I fell at least twice. I stopped counting how many times I tripped. I figured we were pretty safe in here, but we still moved as silently as possible, considering all the gear we were carrying. The flashlights went away before we came to the street and we picked up the pace as we cut across McDonald Ave. and down Seeley Street. At least, that's what the long fallen street sign said it was. We crossed into another park, using the roads this time so as to not have to pull out the flashlights again. I began hearing voices off in the distance and after a minute spotted the fires that they were gathered around. They were far enough off, that I wasn't worried about them. They sounded like they were drunk, so I was betting they weren't one of Riley's search parties. Sticking to the road helped us pick up time and kept me from getting more banged up than I already was. I felt my gut tense up as we came to the uncertainty at the other side.

We turned onto Bedford Ave. walking straight down the middle of the street. I noticed that there were many more people out at this time of night than back home. There wasn't much to do back in the Boston area after the sun went down, at least not in my little suburb. I'd have to ask Hags, if and when I saw him again, how the nightlife is in the city proper. Here, it was like you saw in the movies, fifty-five gallon drums with fires burning inside them, while people stood around either passing a bottle, or just chatting. We passed maybe ten to twelve people in the course of a mile or so. None of them seemed to be all that interested in us. They just kept to themselves and made sure we weren't coming too close. I'm sure they all had weapons, but they also seemed to be ordinary folks. We came to a major cross street, which seemed to be a sort of hub of activity. I saw the first electric lights since we left the park on the corner. It was a spotlight mounted over a door and was lighting up the section of street in front of a building. I could hear the small generator humming next to the stoop.

There was another drum fire burning off to the side and what looked to be an older couple of men sitting on the stairs, while two others sat a couple feet away in old kitchen chairs, at a makeshift table playing chess. I smiled and told the others to stay in the shadows on the other side of the street. I motioned for Drake to come with me and we slung our rifles, slowly walking toward the men with our hands up in the air.

"You do realize they're gonna be nasty, or run away right?" Drake asked.

"Probably," I said.

"Then why're we doing this again?" I stopped for a moment to look at him.

"I'm giving it another shot, because I'd like to know what is up ahead of us, and if anyone has been looking for us this far away from the battle site. I'm sure they've already seen us. They haven't run off yet, and they weren't staring us down. I figure they may be the only people that WILL talk to us," I said.

"Can't hurt, unless they're with Riley and have a radio to tell him where we are," he mumbled.

"Keep talking, you're making me want to find Riley and his men, just so I have someone to kill beside you," I said with a smirk. I heard him chuckle as we got closer.

We were about fifteen feet away, when I heard one of them say, "You can put your hands down. We can see you're not carrying anything in them."

"Thanks," I said, shielding my eyes from the bright spotlight shining right at us.

"What can we do for ya?" One of the men at the little table asked without looking up at us.

"We have a map and were just passing through, but I figured we should probably find out if there are any roads that are impassable ahead of us," I asked, leaning on the railing of the stairs, my back to the spotlight.

"What's your name?" The old man at the table asked.

"Mack and this is my friend Drake," I answered.

"Well hello Mack and Drake. I'm Eli, this is Joseph across from me, David and Will are on the stairs," he said with a nod to the other men. Eli was the oldest looking of the group. He had grey hair that had receded to the middle of his skull and a heavy scruff on his face. He was wearing a battered looking ski jacket, black leather gloves and had a blanket wrapped around his legs and tucked into the kitchen chair.

Joseph was across from him. He was wearing a knit cap, Carhart Jacket and mittens that matched the cap. He had a grey beard and faded blue eyes. "How is it that you're just passing through when there ain't no way into, or out of the city?" Joseph asked, looking very curious, "Or at least there wasn't."

"Well, to be honest we're not coming from out of the city, but I know for a fact that there are ways in and out now," I said.

"I'm guessing this has to do with what happened earlier then huh?" Eli asked, looking us up and down.

"It does," I answered.

"So, you're Riley's men. Listen, we don't want any trouble," he said, reaching into his jacket.

"No no no, we are NOT with Riley, I swear," I said, holding my hands up in front of me.

"Then how do you know what happened earlier?" Will asked. "You're not with the military." His hand rested on the butt of his gun. Will looked younger than the others. He still had salt and pepper hair with a goatee. He was wearing a heavy leather jacket and a beat up old Yankees cap.

"How do you know what happened earlier?" Drake asked.

"We could hear the gunfire. Only Riley and the military have that kind of firepower," Will said.

"Well, we're from Boston. We came here to help get rid of the military. We were working with Riley. He turned on us as soon as we took out the troops on your borders," I said, trying to not sound as angry as it made me feel.

"How'd you get past the military up there, or was Boston not important enough to have troops there?" David asked, grinning.

"No, we had troops, they're gone now. We got rid of them," I answered.

"Of course he turned on ya. I coulda told ya that woulda happened if you'd found me earlier," Eli said.

"Yeah well, the rest of your fine New Yorkers neglected to tell us that when we ran into them a couple days ago," Drake said, sitting on the steps next to Will who had now relaxed a bit.

"'course they did, they're terrified of Riley," Joseph said.

"And you're not?" I asked, taking out a cigarette from the case and lighting it.

"Hah! It'd take a colder day in hell than this, before I'm afraid of some punk like Riley," Joseph said.

"The four of us are vets. We all served together through a hell that most people can't even comprehend. Gonna take more than Riley to scare us," David said proudly. He was wearing an old Army jacket, tattered jeans, combat boots and some wool mittens.

"Gimme one of those, kid," Eli said, smiling and holding his hand out to me. I returned the smile, opened the case again and gave him one of the five cigarettes I had left.

"I'm gonna call the rest of my team over, if that's okay with you. It looks like we may be here for a bit, if you don't mind talking to us," I said, motioning for the rest of Alpha.

"Fine by us, but it sounds like you should be talking to the resistance instead of us," Eli said, giving me a go ahead wave.

"Resistance?" Drake asked.

"Yeah, us old men aren't the only ones that wanna stand up to Riley. They just don't have the numbers yet is all," Will said.

"Yeah, we're gonna need to know more about this resistance if that's okay," I said, raising an eyebrow.

Eli and his friends told us everything they knew. There was a small group of maybe two to three hundred men and women that were working on ousting Riley out of power. The group had only gotten more organized in the last few months. Riley, on the other hand had been consolidating his power for a few years now. He had started out as a mid level gangster type. After the storm he had risen quickly, dispatching his competition and taking over their power bases. It seems that New York City had been embroiled in a turf war for over three years. Then the military showed up and tried to bull their way in, like they did everywhere. By then, Riley had enough men to give the military a decent fight to try and keep control of HIS city.

All Riley wanted was the city though. He seemed to have little care for the people living here. Only the people who worked for him got any of the benefits. Everyone else had to scrounge for food and supplies at the tiny shops he set up. Anyone dumb enough to openly oppose him were dealt with quickly and sometimes very publicly. Will told us a story about how Riley had taken care of a group of people that tried to wrest control from him a couple years ago. He had them strung up from old light poles lining the main street in the neighborhood they had lived in.

We stayed off to the side of the stoop, while Eli and his friends filled us in. They had said that they hadn't seen any of Riley's men driving around the area in the last few hours, but they had been by early in the day, just a couple hours after they had heard the gunfire. I eventually saw a curtain move in one of the buildings across the street. It took a minute or two, but I finally caught someone peeking out the window. I quietly mentioned it to Eli and he laughed and waved me off. "That's just Marvin's wife Jane, her hobby is spying and gossiping, she's harmless," he said.

"This is probably true, but we've been here long enough. We have people waiting for us at Mt. Sinai, and we don't want to take the chance of putting any of you in harm's way. You've been incredibly helpful," I said, stepping out of the shadows and shaking Eli's hand. He looked down as he pulled his hand away and saw that I had given him the cigarette case.

"I can't take these from you," he said.

"Think of it as payment for the help sir," I said, smiling at my brave new friend.

We said our goodbye's and Will turned the spotlight off for thirty second while we slipped off and made our way back into the darkness. I was hoping that he had a vehicle for us to borrow, but they used most of their spare fuel for the generator.

It was around midnight by the time we left Eli and his friends. We had taken a right at the intersection they were playing chess at onto Atlantic Ave. Woodsie made a joke saying that he wouldn't pay such a high price for such a run down neighborhood. It took me a minute to figure out that he was talking about the game Monopoly. After I figured that out, it was really funny. We spent the next three hours zigzagging down side streets and across intersections. We stopped every hour or so to check our bearings on the map that Drake was carrying.

I wasn't too afraid of us getting lost though. The one thing that I found that I liked about New York, was that the streets went pretty much in a straight line, unlike Boston. We followed Morgan Ave. north and it brought us out to a different section of Route 278. We hid for a good long time in a deserted gas station. We had seen headlights earlier on our walk, but they were well off in the distance and that had been at least a couple hours ago.

Eventually, I decided we had waited long enough and Drake and I went to go take a look. The others seemed happy to get a break from the long hours of walking and lugging their gear. We had taken to switching off carrying Woodsie's M-60 because it was so heavy. I would have gladly left it behind somewhere, but I was pretty sure we were going to need it before long.

Drake and I walked down the street that ran parallel to 278 and soon found a ramp leading up onto the highway itself. Neither of us liked the risks, but we had to know if this would get us closer to the hospital. We walked the half mile down the wide road. Even after all these years, it felt odd to be walking down the middle of a snow covered highway. I heard a sigh and glanced over at Drake. I couldn't really see him very well, since it was around 3AM and there wasn't any light anywhere. "What's up?" I asked.

"You can't see that yet?" he asked. "Wow, your eyes are going in your old age."

"Huh?" I said, looking forward. "Oh, that, man that blows," The road was covered with snow, even though there was no light you could distinctly see where the snow ended and became an inky black. We finished walking to the edge and saw that at some point in the last five years the bridge crossing this section of the city had fallen in on itself, or been blown up, like the bridges in Boston had been.

I kicked snow off the edge and watched it fall the first forty feet, or so before I lost it in the dark. Drake was looking at the map and within a minute he had an "ah hah" moment. He tugged on my long wool coat and pointed to a small road, just a bit further ahead, that seemed to cross over as well. I smiled and gave him a nod as we trekked back to the others at the gas station.

Tom and Jim had fallen asleep while we were gone. Woodsie and Eric both jumped when we called out that we were coming ahead. We gave Tom and Jim five minutes to wake up before we headed out to what the map called Greenpoint Ave. It was about a half a mile from where we were and seemed to go across the same stretch of water. We got to the intersection and Drake told us it was time to turn. We moved silently at this point. This area seemed to be a much more industrial section of the city and there weren't a lot of places to hide.

We spread out across the street, so that we couldn't all be taken out in one burst of fire and made our way carefully forward. Up ahead, I could see the road rise in the air and figured we were close to the bridge. There didn't seem to be any of Riley's men here, but they could be close by. I knew if it had been me, I would have shut down every access point out of this small section of town. It would be much easier to find a group of people, if you knew they were confined in a certain area. Maybe, he wasn't as smart as I thought he was.

There was no one covering the small bridge and we crossed with no problems. We came across what used to be Route 495 and I made a joke about following it home. We crossed Queens Blvd. I noticed that the nightlife had indeed finally turned in. Guess you couldn't call it the city that never sleeps anymore. We crossed a gigantic rail yard. Drake saw headlights nearby and we held up in one of the cars for twenty minutes to make sure whoever was driving around was long gone.

Out of the rail yard, we found an old Subway to hide out in. The street in front of us would lead us to a bridge that dumped us near the hospital. Drake laid out the map on the dusty old counter. "Whatta ya think?" he asked after a minute.

"I think the chances of that bridge being intact all the way across, are slim to none," I answered.

"Even if it is, Riley HAS to have guys there," Tom said.

"If he doesn't, then I am seriously overestimating the man, I underestimated earlier," I said, shrugging.

"If we don't go this way it's a long trip to the next way across," Drake said, pointing to a spot on the map.

"What about a boat?" Jim asked.

"You got one hidden in your ass?" Woodsie asked.

"Not today, but it looks like there could be docks there," he said, pointing to some small buildings along the shore.

"They look industrial and I myself have no idea how to drive a big ass boat," I said, looking around to see if anyone else did.

"It's a good idea though. I say we cut across and make our way to the shoreline to see if we can find a smaller boat. If we go from here to here it's only about a half a mile," Drake said pointing at two small areas on the map, "We could even use an engine. It's far enough away from the bridges that we'd be long gone before they got to either point."

"Sounds like a plan. Now, let's just hope they haven't got men there," I said, trying to sound hopeful.

"Or that it's not frozen over," Eric said.

We made our trip a little more complicated than we had to. I didn't like the idea of staying on one street too long after we left the bridge. We zigzagged across until we saw the huge docks. We snuck our way through the old warehouses and down to the water itself. Thankfully, Eric was wrong and it wasn't frozen over. I was thinking there may be a tugboat or something that we could use here, but it seemed I was wrong as well.

Making our way back out to the road, we ran parallel to the water, looking for any signs of a smaller dock. We lucked out while passing through a State park. There were deserted boats on trailers and vehicles all around the small dock. It seems that after the storm hit, no one felt like recreational fishing. It took a few minutes, but we found one that had a little bit of gas in it. It wasn't big enough for all of us though, which meant finding at least one more workable engine.

The rest of us set to looking for another boat, while Drake checked out the engine that had fuel in it. I almost jumped out of my skin every time he tried starting it. At first, I thought there was no way it would work, sounding the way it did. It soon stopped making the sickening huffing it had been making and turned over. "How the hell did you manage that?" I asked as he turned off the motor.

"Just cleaned off the plugs and it started fine," he said, smiling.

"Good, now do the same for this one," Tom said as the rest of Alpha pushed a trailer with a second boat on it.

Within twenty minutes Drake had the second engine running as well. It didn't sound as smooth as the first, but it would have to do. We made sure both boats had oars in them, in case the engines died, and split into two groups. We had to hurry, the sun would be up in an hour or so, and the sky was already beginning to lighten. In a way that was a blessing as well, none of us were experienced boat captains and the idea of driving a boat for the first time in the pitch black, didn't seem all that intelligent. Then again, the whole idea seemed only slightly more intelligent.

Drake drove one boat with me and Woodsie, while Jim took the helm of the second boat. Jim had said that he had owned a boat long ago when he lived in Florida for a few years. Drake insisted that we call him Captain as we pulled away from the dock. The engines seemed deafening as we slid across the water. Even with the lightening sky, we almost hit some rocks off the shore of the island between the two land masses. The trip we had plotted was just slightly over a half mile in almost a straight line. It dragged on, what seemed like forever, with the racket we were making.

As we passed through the channel, I caught sight of headlights off to my right. They looked to be suspended from midair. "That has to be the other bridge we were looking at," I said, tapping Drake on the shoulder and leaning close so he could hear me.

"At least we know it's intact now," he chuckled.

"And well covered," I said, counting at least four pair of headlights," I added.

"I think they heard us," Woodsie said point to the bridge.

I could only see the headlights flashing as they moved to turn around. They were heading back over the bridge and coming to find us, "We should probably move now," I yelled into Drakes ear as he nodded and opened up the throttle. I was motioning to Jim in the other boat, and after a few seconds, I heard his engine cycle up a notch as well.

Having never docked a boat before, Drake essentially drove us slowly into the large commercial docks. He found a set of stairs that came down close enough to the water that we could climb up onto them. We pulled as close as we could. Thankfully, Woodsie's arms were long enough to grab a hold of a railing. We let the boat float off, while we helped Tom and the others out of their boat. "We saw the guys on the bridge drive off. We should scoot, now," Tom said.

"Agreed," Jim said, nodding as we jogged around the huge warehouse and onto the road leading us out of the complex.

We moved quickly down E91st Street until it came to 3rd Street. I still hadn't heard or seen any cars as we turned right. We trotted down a few blocks and then cut across until we got to Lexington Ave. We traveled down Lexington, for seven or eight blocks then turned left. We finally saw headlights off to our left. We held up for a minute or two, before crossing Park Ave. Ducking into what looked a like a college campus building, I pulled out my radio and flipped it on.

"Baby bear to Papa bear," I said.

"Hold one," I heard Gomez say.

"It's about time you got here," George hissed, "Your wife has been driving me nuts!"

"Sorry, we made as good a time as we could," I replied.

"Where are you?" he asked.

"We're close," was all I gave him.

"We need to get you in here, pronto," he said.

"How's it looking out there?" I asked.

"Bad, very bad, we're surrounded, but they stay far enough back that we can't get a shot at too many of them without exposing ourselves. Unfortunately, they're close enough that if we step outside they know it and try to mow us down," he said with a sigh.

I thought for a minute and keyed the mic, "Alright, what I need you to do is, get some people up on the southern side of the building and keep them occupied. When I give a yell, make sure the front doors open. It's gonna be tricky, but it should work if they don't know we're here," I said.

"That sounds a bit more than tricky," he said.

"It's all I got at the moment," I replied.

"It's your ass," he said, "Give me a few minutes, when you here the firing start, give it a minute, then go."

"You DO know what side is south right?" I asked.

"The one pointing down on the map right?" he said, "Of course I do, now do what you're told and get in here in one piece."

"Copy that, see you soon," I said.

"That's the big plan?" Eric asked. "Run fast and hope they don't shoot us?"

"Again, do you have a better plan?" I replied.

"No, but I could probably come up with one in a couple minutes," he said, sounding annoyed.

"You work on that then. In the meantime, get ready to run really, really fast," I said, smiling at him.

"How have you survived this long?" Eric asked.

"Good genes," I said with a wink.

We were checking our gear and ammo when we heard the firing start slightly off in the distance. We snuck to the edge of the street and bolted across, into a small park like area. We slowed down, ducking behind trees and staying spread out a bit. After about thirty seconds, we saw some of Riley's men run toward the gunfire. A few seconds later, more of them ran right by us, heading to the ruckus. I gave it another ten count, flipped on the radio and gave everyone a nod, "You three go first. Drake and I will bring up the rear. When you get to the door turn and give us covering fire, if you can," I said as I took one last quick look around, "GO!"

The three of them took off running as the rattling of small arms fire got louder. The rest of Riley's men had taken up positions near George's side of the building. I heard a .60 chugging away from above as well. **"OPEN THEM, NOW!"** I yelled into the radio as I nodded to Drake and we bolted for the doors. Woodsie reached the doors first, just as someone inside opened them. He spun training his M-60 in the direction of the incoming fire and let loose. Jim was kneeling behind him as Eric took over holding the door.

I was in front of Drake and hit the door first. Tapping both men on the shoulder as I went by, so they knew it was okay to come inside. Drake ran by them as well and inside. I heard Woodsie whoop as two of our troops closed and sealed the large doors up again, now that we were inside and safe. George was directly in front of me with a wide grin. He threw his arms open and stepped forward to give me a hug. I laughed as he lifted me off the ground and gave me a sloppy kiss on the cheek.

"Hey Mack," I heard Drake say softly behind me.

"Yeah buddy, what's up?" I asked as I spun to see him. I stopped suddenly, tilting my head to the side, like a dog listening to a distant sound.

"Drake," I said, stepping toward him, "What's wrong?" He was pale and for the first time in forever, I saw a foreign look on his face, fear. His eyes met mine, then they glanced down. Mine followed, and saw his hand covering his stomach. His hand moved, the blood began flowing more rapidly, covering his filthy shirt.

**"JESUS!"** I said, running toward him. His knees buckled and I caught him as he toppled over.

"I think we shoulda ran faster bro," he said as he laid his head on my shoulder. I could hear George screaming for a medic, but I didn't care and began screaming as well. I scooped his nearly lifeless body up into my arms as I stood. He groaned in pain as I turned to go to the infirmary. "Things were just starting to get good too," Drake said, laying his head on my shoulder. George was still screaming for a medic as I stumbled by him.

## Chapter 11

I paced outside the small room where they were working on Drake. Looking down, I saw the blood smeared on my hands and shirt. He had been in there for what seemed like forever, but it probably wasn't more than half an hour. Chris had come out at one point, to tell me that his wound was a through and through and that he had a good chance of being okay. The docs were more worried about a perforated bowel, or intestine and infection than the actual wound. None of it made me feel any better.

George steered me toward a sofa and sat me down. He was standing in front of me talking, yet sounded like he was a mile away. I couldn't get Drakes last words out of my head, "Things were just starting to get good too," he had said as I carried him through the building. He was a month or two away from being a dad for the first time. Along with the fact, that we had discovered Kelly, his old fiancée, that we all thought was dead, was very much alive and well.

After the Battle of the Mass Ave. Bridge the clans had a much closer relationship. Chris and I had heard about a school teacher in Boston named Kelly when we first met Hags and his people. We were short on time right then to investigate it, but once things calmed down, we made a few trips into town, without Drake knowing. To find out what was what. It seems that she had been excited as well when she had heard that there were survivors in Menotomy. According to Hags, she had been asking questions about us too. Our first meeting was very private. Hags had told us where she lived and that she'd be expecting us. She swung open the door and quickly dragged us inside to be smothered in hugs and kisses. Tears flowed freely at the sight of her. I'd like to say that only the girls cried, but I'd be lying if I didn't admit that I shed a few as well. We had all been so close back in the day. It was amazing that she was still alive after all these years.

The first ten minutes, or so were tear soaked and strange. We couldn't stop hugging or touching each other, almost as if the touching solidified that the other was truly real. Once we all calmed a bit, we sat and she told us her story. She had been a teacher on the south shore of Massachusetts and had a long commute from her place with Drake in Medford. She had gone to work the day of the storm, it was after all, a day like any other. The meteors hit on her commute home. She had gotten north of Quincy when the smaller one hit that wiped out most of Rhode Island and Cape Cod. Her car had been rocked by the shockwave and she had been knocked out cold. She had no idea how long she had been out for, but it was dark by the time she awoke. Someone was reaching around her, trying to undo her seatbelt. She remembered screaming and attempting to fight them off. Come to find out, they were trying to free her from her wreck of a car. Most had been killed in the shockwave, she had been lucky enough to be pinned in by two semi trailers that absorbed a lot of the shockwave. Even with all the protection, she had a shattered right leg, as well as a broken clavicle and vertebrae near the top of her back. Her memory was patchy after that, remembering only bits and pieces through the haze of pain, of some of her saviors carrying her, until they found some help. She cried a lot telling us the story of how useless she felt, while all the other survivors worked so hard to find food and supplies to help keep her alive.

It took months for her to heal up and another month, or so to really be able to walk around well. She stayed with the survivors, which were now some of her closest friends, but she never forgot us. Her and the others would have long conversations about exploring the city. About trying to get to the towns north of it, but in all the time she had been recovering, none of them had heard a peep from anywhere north of Boston. No one was even sure it was still there. After that, the first winter kicked in and things got really bad for everyone. Things just sort of slipped away and she had been busy trying to rebuild her life. Seth, her husband of two years, had been the man reaching around her the day of the storm trying to free her from the wreck.

It took her another forty minutes to finish catching us up on the last few years. Then she stood and smiled softly at us. She told us to hold on a minute as she ducked out of the room. She returned and made us close our eyes before she entered. When we opened them, she was standing behind a small boy. Chris, instantly started bawling again. My mouth dropped open and you could have knocked me over with a feather. He was about five or six years old and had blond curly hair with bright, shining blue eyes, like his father. I smiled wide and asked him his name. He told me it was Matthew and I nodded slowly as I looked up at his mother who was blushing, a bright, crimson red.

She nodded ever so slightly to me. Chris heard his name and cried even harder. Matthew was Drake's middle name.

The girls chatted for awhile and I got to know her little man a bit better. None of us mentioned the similarities openly, but we didn't really need to. By the time we left, I had become Uncle Mack and little Matt looked at Chris funny, because she wouldn't stop hugging him. Kelly sent him back to his room just before we left and she confirmed our suspicions. She also told us that her husband knew the truth, but she'd rather not tell Matthew yet. We both agreed and said our goodbye's which were almost as tear filled as the hellos.

Our next trip was with Drake. We didn't tell him beforehand and brought him along under some silly lie I don't remember. Thinking about it in hindsight, I probably should have warned him. He saw Kelly when she opened the door and crumpled like a house of cards. He stood slowly to hug her and in no time was holding her around her waist as he cried. His face buried in the nape her neck. He had been so lost without her for so long, that there were times I truly thought it would kill him. Chris and I left them alone for a bit, but she asked us to rejoin them before she disappeared out of the room like last time.

Drake was still in a perpetual state of shock, staring at me blankly in disbelief. I smiled as I squeezed his shoulder and told him to hold on. When she came back into the room, I watched the rest of the blood drain from his face. After a moment, she quietly introduced him to a smaller, almost identical version, of himself. He croaked out a "Hello there," and gulped. If I didn't know him better, I'd have thought he was about to pass out.

Drake knelt in front of the small child and examined his features, feeling around like a blind person. Matthew stood, unafraid, at this new person and seemed completely comfortable, almost instantly. Drake stood, nodding slowly. He put his large hand on top of Matt's head and smiled down at him before looking to Kelly, who had her hand pressed against her mouth, holding back more tears. "You did good," was all Drake said to her about the matter, while the child was in the room. Matt made his way over to me and we play fought for a bit, before his mother asked him to go to his room for a few minutes. Once he was gone, Drake hammered Kelly with questions about Matt. To her credit, she answered them all honestly. He sat silently for a few minutes, absorbing what he had just discovered; it was a lot all at once. When he was done, he agreed that telling Matt at this time, wasn't going to do anything beside cause confusion. He told her that he would like him to know eventually, and she agreed that it was a good idea. For the moment, Drake was okay with being Uncle Drake. I knew him well enough to know that it wouldn't always be acceptable, but for now, it was okay.

He had told Kelly about Sam and when he got home, he told Sam about Kelly as well. Sam took the news well and genuinely seemed excited when she heard about Matt. She wanted to know all about him, and since he was going to have a little half brother or sister soon, figured that she should meet him sooner, rather than later. Drake agreed and a couple weeks later he did bring her in town to meet them both. Chris and I stayed out of that one, but he assured me things went better than he could have ever expected. He also met Seth that day as well. Amazingly enough, I only caught the faintest whiff of jealousy from Drake. He never did like sharing what he thought was his.

Now, he was laying in an operating room, possibly dying and all he really wants, is to live long enough to spend some time with his kids. One he never knew he had and the other that hadn't been born yet. I rubbed my grubby hands over my stubble covered face and sighed heavily. He had been so happy the last few weeks before we left Boston. He was making frequent trips in town, reconnecting with Kelly and getting to know Matt. He would bring Sam and they would make a day of it. He hadn't seemed so normal or happy in years. He was right. It was just starting to get good for him. I hope it doesn't all come crashing to an end.

I was brought out of my reverie, when I felt someone sit next to me. Out of the corner of my eye I saw Eva as she laid her head on my shoulder. "I just heard, is he gonna be okay?" she asked.

"I dunno yet, but they think so," I answered. Looking around, I noticed that it was darker in here and I saw the camping lanterns set along the walls. "They shut the power off?" I asked Eva.

"Yeah, like yesterday sometime," she said.

"That's okay I suppose. It was more of a luxury anyway," I said, shrugging. "I gotta find George."

"He's probably up in the command center," she said, looking up at me with a sad face.

"Can you do me a favor and stay here?" I asked.

"Of course honey," she answered. "Anne is on her way down too, so she'll keep me company."

"Excellent, thank you, come find me if they tell you anything okay?" I said, giving her a kiss on the forehead.

"You know it." I heard her say as I walked down the hallway toward the main foyer.

I found George pacing around the command center. Gomez was sitting at the radio talking with someone, probably one of the sentries. I heard an audible gasp from off to my right as I walked in. Hags, Brett and Art were sitting at a table over in the corner. George stopped pacing to stare at me, as if I were the grim reaper himself. "I don't have any news yet, last I knew they were hopeful," I said as I took a seat at the table.

"Good," was all George said as he returned to pacing, he was chewing on an already stubby fingernail as well.

"God Mack, I'm glad you're back and okay," Hags said.

"I'd say I'm pretty mother fuckin' far from okay, but thanks," I said.

"How many men do we have left here?" I glanced around the room.

"Only a few hundred," George answered.

"You wanna be a little more fucking specific?" I growled.

"Mack?" Brett asked at my sudden anger.

"Yes, Brett?" I said, seething.

"A bit harsh maybe?" Brett said,sounding just a tad too condescending for my taste and off I went.

"You think so Brett, cuz I don't. I just spent two days running for my life after watching two hundred and twenty-seven of my friends die. Yeah, I know exactly how many of them there were. So I really don't think it's asking too much for you idiots **TO REMEMBER HOW MANY ARE STILL FUCKING ALIVE!**" I screamed.

"Three hundred and fifteen," I heard Gomez say calmly from behind me, "That's counting you, Alpha and Drake, if he lives. If not it'd be three hundred and fourteen."

"Thank you Gomez," I said with a sigh of relief, "You wanna take George's job?" I asked.

"Nahh, I don't like Twinkies or Buffy that much," he said without hesitation.

I smiled a little at his remark and continued, "Alright, now that I know how many people we have, I'm gonna need to know how much food and ammo we have as well. I also need to see a map of where we think they're stationed. Let's get it together folks. We need to get the fuck out of here, so I can go kick that fucker's ass."

"Mack, you should probably get some sleep and maybe wash up a bit," Brett said.

"After I have all that info I'll think about it. I won't be able to relax until I have a full briefing, so we may as well get on with it. The quicker it's done the quicker we can figure this out," I said.

The next couple hours, were spent going over all the numbers and getting everyone on the same page. All the team leaders that were left were gathered up. We all met in the command center with George and the other leaders. Come to find out, we were okay for a few more days as long as we didn't have a lot of protracted fire fights with the goons held up outside. I still hadn't figured much of anything out, but I was as caught up as anyone else was.

I had gone to one of the rooms with a bed in it to clean up a bit and have some time to myself to sort things out in my head. I had left word with everyone where I was so Eva or Anne could find me with an update on Drake. I closed the heavy wooden door and put my back against it. My adrenaline was starting to wane. Suddenly, I was exhausted and sore. I pushed myself off the wall and stripped off my shirt. I washed up with the bucket of water and a cloth that were on the edge of the sink. Catching a glimpse of my red rimmed, bloodshot eyes in the mirror, made me stop and stare into it for a minute.

A week's worth of growth on my face along with some bruises and old scars, coupled with the suit cased sized bags under my eyes, made me look old and battered. I rubbed my eyes and all I could see in my head was Drake on a cold slab. I was terrified that something was going to happen to my oldest and closest friend. I tried to preoccupy myself with getting washed up, but his pale face kept popping into my head.

I sat in the chair next to the bed and untied my boots as visions of Sam and Kelly ran through my brain. They were wailing and screaming at me, "This is your fault! Why'd you let him die!" over and over again. I knew they wouldn't react that way and shook my head, trying to get rid of the horrid visuals. I undid my belt and dropped my grime covered pants to the floor before climbing into the bed. It was cold, but the pillow felt amazing under my head. The visions returned as soon as my eyes closed. Even with them, I was asleep in under three minutes.

Eva woke me later, I have no idea how long I was out, but it was still dark. She told me that Drake was alive and resting comfortably. I hugged her tight and gave her a kiss on the cheek before I dropped myself back onto the pillow. She also told me that George had sent a message with her and that everything was quiet for the time being. I mumbled a, "thank you," and heard her giggle before she kissed me on the nose and pulled the blankets up around my neck. I was asleep so fast that I don't remember her leaving the room.

By the time I woke up again, the sun had come up. Everything was still grey, just not as dark as it was at night. I got out of bed, stretched and took a piss. After that, I stood in the empty room trying to fully wake up. I shrugged and dropped to the floor to start my normal morning routine. It used to be that my mornings started the same way every day, a cup of coffee and a couple cigarettes while sitting on my porch. That all ended after the storm. Now, most mornings started with sit-ups, push-ups, and chin-ups. It wasn't that I necessarily enjoyed working out in the morning, but I wasn't getting any younger. The way life was these days, if you were slower or softer than the next guy, you didn't last long. Another reason to work out in the morning was that the cold made everything stiffen up at my age, and not in a good way. Working out helped loosen up the muscles and get the body warm. Roy, Teddy and Liam worked out religiously. Roy had almost fifteen years on me and he could outrun me any day of the week. I at least had a higher pain and cold threshold than he did. It's amazing the stupid things that you learn about people when you spend way too much time being bored with them.

I washed up, got dressed and went to check on Drake. The nurse told me he was still resting, but that he seemed to be doing well. I thanked her and made my way to the command center. George was there with Gomez and Art. Hags and Brett hadn't showed up yet. George gave me a smile as I entered. He nodded toward a pot of coffee and some mugs. I nodded back and gave him a wink as I made myself what may be the last fresh coffee I get to taste. "Feeling a bit more human?" he asked as he sat down at the table across from me.

"Slightly," I answered, sipping at the hot coffee. "Drake is still out, but they say he should be okay," I said.

"Yep, I have someone update me hourly," he said with a grin, "He isn't just your friend y'know."

"True," I said.

"We really need to figure out how to get the fuck out of this. They're not just gonna continue to sit out there peacefully," George said, scratching at his neck.

"No they're not. I'm expecting Riley sometime today. He's let us sweat long enough, and by now he knows I'm here," I said.

"Yeah, about all that, you okay?" George asked.

"What, about feeling responsible as I watched hundreds of my men get mowed down by some lunatic, while I had to run away and not save any of them. Is that what you're asking about?" I said only, sounding slightly sarcastic.

"Yeah about that," George said, looking squeamish.

"Yeah, I'm nowhere near okay, about any of that. I will send you all home and stay here alone, if that's what it takes for me to kill this fucker," I said bluntly.

"You know we wouldn't leave without you," he said.

"Then I guess we'd better get to work on how to take him out then. That way we can all go home." I shrugged.

We spent awhile catching each other up. A bit later Brett and Hags showed up and we got to do the same with them. Around noon, Teddy came into the command center and said he needed to see me and George. "What's up?" I asked as we stepped out into the hall.

"Um, it seems you have a visitor," Teddy said.

"Told you Riley would show up," I said.

"No, it's not outside, and it's not Riley," Teddy said, leading us down the hall to a closed door.

"Teddy, no one got in here, Gomez or I would've heard about it," George said, looking perplexed.

"Yeah well, I guess we need to work on our security a little better," he said, swinging open the door. Inside was a face I never thought I'd see again.

"Sampson!" I said, rushing inside.

"Hey there Mack, you look worse than the last time I saw you," he said, smiling as he stood from behind the small table and shook my hand. His huge hand swallowed mine up as he stepped close and gave a quick hug as well.

"Who the fuck's this?" George asked.

"George, this gigantic bastard is Sampson. I met him when he dragged me out of the shop," I said, grinning.

"He's military?" George said, stiffening visibly.

"Not anymore sir. After I saw, and understood, what they were doing up in Boston, I decided to leave the Army as soon as I could. Once we got back here, I didn't re-up. It just wasn't worth it," Sampson said. He towered over everyone in the room. He was around six foot four and had shoulders almost as broad. He had long, dark brown, unruly hair and a heavy scruff, almost beard on his face.

"They said they found him outside the boiler room in the basement. I don't really care who he is, I just wanna know how he got in here?" Teddy asked.

Sampson started to answer and I put up a hand for him to stop, "I'm gonna guess from his pants and his smell that he came in through the sewers," I said with a smirk.

"BINGO!" Sampson said before he let out a deep full laugh.

"How'd you know where we were?" I asked, pulling out the other chair and taking a seat.

"A couple of birds told me... very old, grumpy birds," he said, smiling.

"Eli told you?" I asked.

"Yep," he answered.

"Why did he tell you?" George asked.

"Well, he didn't tell me specifically," Sampson said, "he sent a message to the resistance."

"Ahh, so you're with them now," I said, nodding slowly.

"Oh no, I AM them. I started it once I got back," he said proudly.

"Well shit, ain't that a kick in the head," I said, glancing up at George who looked stunned.

"I heard about your men, I am really sorry," he said, his eyes locked on mine.

"Thank you, I'm sure it'll hit me eventually. Right now though, there's far too many of us left for me to mourn," I said flatly.

"That's why I'm here, to offer our assistance," Sampson said.

"Can you get us all out of here through the sewer?" George asked.

"I suppose we could over the course of a couple days, but you have a good amount of men," Sampson said, scratching his scruff. "We can get smaller groups out though and lead you safely through the city."

"So you could get me near Grand Central?" I asked, a plan starting to form in my head.

"Near it, hell I can get you in it. There are tons of access points in the tunnels around Grand Central," he said, grinning.

"You really think he's gonna just let you walk in there and kill him?" George asked, looking at me as if I was insane.

"No, I'm sure he has security in the tunnels. I'm not gonna underestimate him again," I said, shaking my head.

"But you're gonna try it anyway aren't you?" George asked, sounding tired.

"Possibly," I said. "In the mean time, if we can impose on your hospitality, we could use some ammo and supplies," I said, turning my attention to Sampson.

"We can do that. I'll go back to get some supplies and men, you figure out what you wanna do. I'll be back later this evening and we can get to work," he said, shaking my hand again.

"Wait here for a few, I'll grab Gomez. He can walk you down to the tunnel and give you a list of stuff we need on the way," I said before walking back out into the hallway. I snapped my fingers, spun, opened the door and ducked my head inside, "Thank you so much Sampson, it was looking pretty bleak until you showed up."

"Oh, it still may be downright dismal, we're nowhere near out of this yet," he said, grinning.

I jogged down the hall to the command center. I grabbed Gomez and explained what I needed as I brought him down to the room. He assured me that he would take care of things. I clapped him on the shoulder before I headed back down the hall to catch up with George. "This could be a very nice turn of events," I said, feeling hopeful.

My heart dropped, as I heard a tinny voice coming from outside **"Oh MAAACCCKKK,"**

"You were saying?" George said as he rolled his eyes.

"Wow, what the fuck? Can't a guy get a break?" I asked to no one in particular. The tinny voice was Riley with a bull horn outside. I had been expecting him, just not right on top of Sampson's arrival. **"I KNOW YOU'RE IN THERE. WHY DON'T YOU COME ON OUT AND WE CAN TALK."**

"Don't even consider going out there," George said when he could tell I was deep in thought.

"Yeah, no, but we may be able to end this quickly if I can get a shot at him," I said as I grabbed a rifle from one of the guys guarding the door. I ran toward the stairs and took them two at a time until I was

117

on the third floor. I found a dark window and peered outside. I grumbled to myself, when I saw his Caddy sitting right out front with just the end of the bull-horn sticking out of the barely cracked window. I opened the window just a few inches anyway. I rested the barrel on the ledge and peered down the sights. No way could I make this shot, the angle was all wrong. I pulled the rifle back in, closed the window and sat with my back against the wall thinking.

**"I'M STILL WAITING MACK."** I heard, coming from downstairs.

I growled as I stood. I jogged back downstairs and handed the rifle back to the guard. **"I'M NOT LEAVING UNTIL I SEE YOUR SMILING FACE."** Riley said, mockingly.

"God, I can't wait to kill him," I said, stalking over to the barricaded doors.

George grabbed me by the shoulder, "Again Mack, you are NOT going out there," he said.

"No, I'm not. I'm homicidal, not suicidal," I said.

I heard footfalls behind me, "What's with all the racket?" Brett said. I turned to find Brett, Hags and Art had come out of the command center.

"Riley's here and he supposedly wants to talk," George said.

**"C'MON MACK, DON'T MAKE ME BURN THIS WHOLE BLOCK DOWN JUST TO TALK TO YOU. YOU HAVE MY WORD THAT YOU WON'T BE HARMED."** Riley's voice grated on me.

"George, we have men up top right?" I asked, glancing at my friend.

"Yeah, I have snipers on the roof and a few floors below it," he answered.

I caught movement and saw Brett walking toward the barricade. "Um Brett, where ya goin?" I asked.

"He said he just wants to talk. I'd rather hear what he has to say, instead of having him set fire to the place," Brett said.

"You're not going out there, he just going to kill you," I said.

"He said you wouldn't be harmed, he gave his word," Brett said, as if this settled everything.

"He can't be serious," George said with a low whistle.

**"I'M GETTING INPATIENT MACK. DON'T YOU WANT THIS ALL TO BE OVER AND ON YOUR WAY HOME? LET'S TALK."** Riley said.

"Well, he's already said he's not leaving until he sees you. It really should be me going out there though. You may be in command of the troops, but I am actually the head of this coalition," Brett said, seeming to stand a little taller.

**"REALLY?** This is when you're going to pick up the pissing contest?" I said, getting into Brett's face. "Listen, that man out there wants one thing and one thing only, us dead. If you think, for half a second, that going out there is anywhere near sane, then you probably shouldn't be in charge of what you decide to have for lunch, much less a whole group of people," I said, poking him in the chest.

"Stand down General," Brett said.

"Aw Jesus," I heard Hags mumble.

"Brett, now is not the time for this," I said. "Please, just let me handle it."

"No, I have this, I'm the one in command here. It's on me to go talk to him. It'll be fine, he gave us his word," he said to us before he nodded to the guards to open the barricade for him.

**"HE KILLED MORE THAN HALF OUR MEN!"** I screamed.

"Those men followed me here because I asked them too," Brett said calmly.

I spun and threw my hands up in the air, "This has to be one of the stupidest things I have ever seen!" I exclaimed.

"Have some faith Mack, I'll be back soon," he said as he stepped outside. The guards quickly closed the doors, but didn't replace the barricades.

**"MACK I'M WAITING. OH..."** I heard from outside and then silence. Obviously, Riley had noticed that Brett had come out to see him.

We crowded around a window as Brett slowly walked down the stairs with his hands held up in the air to show he didn't have a weapon. Time seemed to slow and there was no sound at all. As he got to the bottom of the stairs I saw his head turn. He smiled and nodded as if to say "See, I was right." He started to walk to the Caddy. He hadn't even gotten to the sidewalk when I heard George yell, "NO!" The report of the rifle came a split second after I saw Brett's head snap to the side. He dropped like a stone. I closed my eyes and shook my head as I let out a curse.

"**MOVE!**" I yelled as I shoved past Art. "George, get me cover!"

I ran toward the doors as I heard George yell into the radio for cover fire. I took a deep breath and bolted outside as I heard my boys lay down a curtain of rounds to help keep me alive a little longer. Art was next to me and we ran down the stairs. It only took a couple seconds, but it seemed an eternity. I saw the window roll down on the Caddy as I grabbed Brett by the front of his shirt and started to drag him up the stairs. Art picked up an arm and made the job much easier. I stared into the darkness and I swear I could see that shark like smile, shining in the back seat, mocking me.

We got to the doors alive. Art finished bringing Brett inside, while I stood in front of them defiantly. My men still rattling off rounds to keep them buttoned up. I glared into the window and could feel him staring back at me. After a moment, the bullhorn reappeared, "**WELL, I GUESS THAT'S THAT THEN**," he said, before rolling the window up as the Caddy slowly drove off.

## Chapter 12

"We really need to get the hell out of here," George said, pacing the length of the table in the conference room. "You heard Riley. He's gonna burn us out of here very soon."

"I agree, not sure how we're gonna get everyone out of here yet, but I agree," I said. I was feeling tired again already and I had only been up for a few hours.

The small conference room was lit by battery powered camping lanterns. The heat had been shut off with the power at least two days ago. It was cold, not unbearably cold, but chilly nonetheless. Art and Hags were here along with me, the team leaders that survived, George and Chris. Sampson was with us as well. He had heard the gunfire and came back as quickly as he could, bringing only minimum supplies and a couple spare men.

"Can we do an evacuation out through the tunnels?" Art asked, glancing over at Sampson who was leaning against the paneled wall.

"We can, it'll be slow going, but it's completely possible. If they figure out what we're doing though, we are completely screwed. There's nowhere to really hide down there," he answered.

"We're just as dead if we stay here any longer," Art said.

"Yeah, we'll get the wounded out first with all medical personnel," I said, looking over at Chris.

"We only have a few seriously wounded, the rest should be able to get themselves out. Drakes gonna be the tough one, but we'll figure it out," Chris said, talking mostly to herself as she wrote a quick list.

"Excellent, as soon as you're finished up with your list, start gathering who you need to help and head toward the boiler room. Gomez can show you where it is," I said.

"Find me or I'll find you before we leave," she said on her way out of the room, it wasn't a request and I knew it.

I'm sure she heard my "Yes dear," as she went out the door.

"Okay, step one is set up. What's next?" George asked. We spent the next hour, or so devising and revising our plan for evacuation. It was quick and dirty, but it sounded feasible and adaptable. We split up to get our plan underway. There was a nice buzz of excitement for the first time since I had been back. Most of these people hated sitting around waiting.

The plan was simple, but effective. Alpha and a small group of men would go with Sampson to run an end around. We would go out through the tunnels and come up behind Riley's men to cause a distraction big enough to buy the evacuation more time. Chris and the others would take the wounded and some supplies with them, out through the tunnels to a warehouse a couple miles away. Riley didn't know where the resistance was hiding, so staying with them would be safe for a short time. There would also be a small contingent of men led by Gomez and Art, that would stay behind defending the hospital, until everyone else was out. They would wait at least a half hour after everyone was gone, so as to hopefully fool Riley's men into believing we were still there. If all went well, Riley would have no idea where we were come nightfall.

It didn't take us long to gear up and get ready. The guards at the lobby doors reported movement and we sent the fire teams up to the upper floors, to hold them off. I could hear the small arms fire off in the distance behind me as I made my way downstairs. Chris had a long line along one wall of the corridor leading into the boiler room. She saw me coming and smiled softly as I hugged her.

"I'll see you in a couple hours?" she asked.

"Of course," I said, plastering on a small smile of my own, before leaning down to give her a quick kiss. "We'll be fine."

"I love you, stay safe," she said as she straightened my harness.

"I love you too," I said with a chuckle as I kissed her on top of her head, before ducking into the boiler room.

Anne was inside with Liam, standing next to a small pile of boxes. I leaned on her shoulder and she smiled up at me. "You ready to get the hell out of here?" I asked her.

"Hell yeah, I always hated New York," she said.

"You need an extra gun?" Liam asked. His arms folded across his chest.

"Taking all the help I can get sir," I said with a nod.

"You gonna be okay if I go with Mack?" Liam asked his wife of over a decade.

"Of course, you go play soldier. Now I'll just worry about both of you," she answered.

"Keep an eye on Drake," I said to her.

"I'm right here you know," I heard him croak from a few feet away.

"Oh I know, I just figured you'd still be asleep," I said, walking over to my old friend. He was dressed and sitting slumped against the wall.

"Nah, they have me pumped full of pain meds though. Seems they can't figure out a way to carry a stretcher down into the sewer, so they need me to get myself down there before they put me back on it," he said, shrugging.

"Man, it's rough being you, they gonna feed you grapes while they carry you?" I said, trying to lighten the mood.

"I asked about that, but they told me that we're outta grapes. Liam said he'd dip his balls in my mouth though, if I really needed him to," Drake said, grinning up at the large man.

"He said he'd get back to me," Liam said deadpan.

"Well, you're with me now, so that'll have to wait until we meet up later," I said with a smirk.

"Sorry bro," Liam said, looking serious.

Drake snapped his fingers in disappointment. He looked up at me and said, "I'll see you in a bit huh?"

"Of course," I said, smiling.

I gave Anne a hug as the rest of Alpha came in. We double checked our gear and gave Sampson the nod. He pulled up the heavy steel plate and waited for us to hop into the rabbit hole. The stench down in the tunnel wasn't nearly as bad as I thought it would be. Then again, I did have a cloth over my nose and mouth. It wasn't there to filter the smell, but it was a pleasant secondary benefit.

There were about twenty five of us down in the tunnels. Alpha along with Roy and Teddy's teams as well as a dozen or so of our regular troops. I would've liked to bring a bigger force, but we were very quickly running out of bodies. Each team had their own resistance guide, so no one got lost. Alpha had gone in first. Each team would give the one in front a one minute head start. It was never a good idea to bunch troops up too much.

The tunnel was dark and dank, some of Sampson's men had lined the wall with lanterns every twenty feet or so. The muck on the floor didn't even come up over the toe of my jump boots, which should make Chris and Anne very happy in a few minutes. We followed the lit tunnel for a hundred yard, before Sampson hooked a right. This side tunnel was more narrow and unlit. He held his lantern over his left shoulder, so we all had some light. "You sure you know where you're goin?" Tom asked as he walked behind the big man.

"I'm pretty sure. Look, if I go up the ladder and get shot, don't follow me. That work for you?" he asked over his shoulder.

"Absolutely," Tom mumbled.

"Think there are rats down here?" Eric asked. "Cuz I really, really hate rats."

"Don't look down is all," Jim said.

"You know what I really, really hate?" Woodsie asked to no one in particular, "I hate Lemurs. Beady eyed little bastards."

"Wait, don't you only see Lemurs in Madagascar?" I asked.

"Yep, that's why I'm proud to be an American," he replied.

I shook my head and kept my mouth shut as I grabbed my radio and keyed the mic. Surprisingly, George could hear me. They had started the evacuation. It would be slow going, until they all got down into the tunnels. He had checked with Gomez and the fighting had intensified topside. Riley's men were starting their push toward the hospital. I checked in with Gomez with my ear bud. He assured me that he was good and the men would hold. "I couldn't be happier to hear that buddy. We'll see you in a little bit," I said to one of the best men I knew.

"We'll be there sir, with bells on," he said.

Another couple hundred yards of walking straight before Sampson led us to the right for a hundred yards or so. Quickly, he took a left turn and picked up his pace. He stopped suddenly and held his lantern up high over his head. It illuminated the rungs of a dingy, old metal ladder that would lead us back up to the street. He turned off the lantern and placed it by his feet before making his slow ascent. "You sure we went out far enough?" Tom asked, looking up at Sampson.

"We're about to find out," Sampson said. He pushed his shoulder up against the heavy man-hole cover. Grunting loudly with the strain, he eased the cover up and quietly slid it back onto the street behind him.

He disappeared through the hole and leaned his head back in, motioning for us to come up. I let everyone go ahead of me and pulled the cover back into place once I reached the top. We moved quickly to cover, in an alley between two nearby buildings. It took me a minute to get my bearings. It should have been easier, considering I could hear the gunfire clearly off in the distance coming from my left.

I checked in with George one more time and he told me that about half of the people were in the tunnels and making their way to the safe house. I let him know we were almost in position and about to kick off our distraction. He wished me luck and I turned off the radio. I gave a nod to Tom and he took point with Sampson, heading off in the direction of the gunfire.

A couple blocks ahead we could see the back side of where Riley's men were. Moving quietly, we took up positions behind a couple burned out cars and got settled in. I was checking the magazine in my AK, when there was a deafening explosion. I dove to the ground and quickly yelled out to make sure everyone was okay. Within ten seconds, everyone had checked in. I sat with my back against the rough metal waiting for my ears to stop ringing.

"What the hell was that?" I asked Sampson, who was still lying on the ground next to me.

"I'd have to say that Riley's got a cannon or two working," he answered, pulling himself up to sit next to me.

"Oh for fuck's sake," I heard Tom say from the car next to us. There was another explosion. This one was a little further away, but almost as loud. I flinched hard. "At least two, and it seems like they have no idea how to aim them either," I said.

"Let's hope they don't figure it out too soon," Eric said.

"Hey Mack," I heard Roy say in my ear, "We're right behind you about to come around the corner, didn't wanna spook you."

"Copy that, come on up, we're all clear for the moment," I said.

"Copy that, we'll set up across the street from you. So, they got a cannon working huh?" he asked.

"At least one," I sighed.

"Fun, be there I a second," Roy said.

The small arms fire from up ahead had tapered off slightly. Once again, there was the deafening explosion and I could see plumes of asphalt and concrete go flying, this time as a shell exploded at the intersection up ahead. They were trying hard to hit the hospital. For the moment, they were falling well short, but it wouldn't be long. I had no idea what cannon they were firing and it was too far away for us to get to it in time. The best I could hope, for was that the hospital was empty before they worked out their targeting problems.

Teddy called when his team came to the corner as well. He had worked with the regular troops and stationed them in some of the upper windows looking over the street in front of the hospital, so it took him a bit longer to meet up with us. He split his team in half. Some of them were on one side of the street with Alpha. The other team, was over with Roy's. I waited for everyone to get set up and looked to both Roy and Teddy. Once they gave me the nod, I glanced quickly at the rest of Alpha. Satisfied that they were as ready as they were gonna be, I took a deep breath and said, "Light 'em up!" The end of that short sentence was lost in a roar of rifle and light machinegun fire. The closest of Riley's men crumpled instantly under the withering fire. We were about sixty yards, or so, away. The first thirty of his men never knew what hit them.

I'd like to say that I was a hardened enough soldier to look at all of this with a certain amount of cold detachment. To a degree, I can say that. I won't say though, that it wasn't gratifying to exact some revenge for all the men that I had lost days before. Part of it felt good, real good actually, and that scared me a little bit. It didn't bother me enough to limit it to one magazine though. I hit the lever on the underside of my AK and dropped out the empty magazine, quickly slamming a new one home.

Riley's men finally figured out what was happening and in under a minute had spun a large group to face us. This helped the men in the hospital as well. They could now fire more openly. Another shell, landed off in the distance. This one was nowhere near as close as the first few. Thankfully, Riley's men didn't seem to be quick learners. Things seemed to be going very well. The boys at the hospital had two groups pinned down and a steady stream of Riley's men were trickling into our line of fire to come help their friends out. We had most of his troops lined up and for a second things felt good.

That feeling disappeared, when I heard Roy yell "Behind!" I spun, slamming my back against the front quarter panel of the car. I saw a dozen men, at least, training their rifles on our positions. I was up in a flash, emptying my new clip at them. I fired in a flurry, hoping to make them dive for cover and buy us a few seconds. I grabbed Eric, who was still firing at the main body of troops in front of us. "We need to move!" I shouted over the rifle fire.

Eric nodded and passed the order along the line. He was up and moving in no time flat. He darted for what looked like a crumbling old parking garage. Tom and the rest of Alpha followed him. I brought up the rear behind Teddy and his men. Roy had moved his group into a small plaza type area on his side of the street as well. Woodsie was chugging away on his 60 from a corner, but the men behind us kept advancing.

I heard Gomez in my ear and stepped away from the firing to hear him better, "What's up?" I asked.

"Buildings on fire boss," he said calmly.

"Well get the fuck out then," I said.

"Yeah, can't yet there's still people leaving," he said. I could hear rifle fire behind him.

"Then fall back and get downstairs to follow them out," I said, getting worried.

"We're good boss, I was just letting you know, cuz I have no idea how long we'll be able to give you support from this side," he said.

Another round landed, this one closer to the hospital. I heard screams as some of the shrapnel took out a bunch of Riley's men. I could hear the second cannon shell whistle before it landed. The detonation shook the ground beneath my feet. It had hit somewhere close, but I couldn't see from inside the garage opening. "Gomez, you listen to Mack and get your men downstairs as soon as possible. We have no idea how structurally sound that building is anymore," I heard George say.

"Teddy, where's our fire support team, these guys are closing on us fast?" I asked Teddy when I glanced outside and saw Riley's men still pushing forward.

"On it Mack," Teddy said, pulling out his radio.

I turned my attention back to Gomez, "Listen, I trust your judgment and all, but you get out of there as soon as you feel you have to, okay? We'll be fine down here."

"Of course boss," Gomez answered, now sounding stressed.

I nodded to myself, "Teddy?" I asked.

"I got nothin' Mack, no answer at all," Teddy said.

"Jesus!" I said, annoyed about the lack of contact.

I heard an explosion behind me and held my breath as I peeked around the edge of the garage opening. Black smoke billowed out of the building next to the hospital. Riley's men were closing from that direction as well. Roy's team were doing their best to hold them back, but it was starting to look like they had forgotten the hospital all together and were just after us. I noticed that Roy looked pressed, but still calm.

"Mack, I still have no word from the fire support," Teddy said as he came up next to me. I started to answer him and was cut off by the next shell landing. The explosion sounded like a roar and I looked to see what had been hit. My jaw dropped as I saw that the hospital had taken a direct shot. It had punched a hole in the side of the building. A large chunk of wall had collapsed with the hit and flames licked quickly up the side of the building. I tried to call Gomez and got no answer. Teddy and I stood, staring at the building, oblivious to everything else until I heard Woodsie yelling behind me that he was almost empty. I shook myself out of my daze, so I could answer him.

My stomach dropped as I heard the next shell hit. It landed with a sickening thud. I was trying to tell Woodsie to calm down and stopped mid sentence when I heard the rumble coming from the hospital. Teddy muttered something next to me and I swiveled my head in time to see the top of the hospital collapse. The roof slid and the building fell in upon itself. Flames and smoke engulfed the bottom half as the rest became rubble. I squeezed my eyes shut and it got hard to breathe. I had to steady myself against the wall. I could hear Roy screaming, in my ear and Teddy next to me, but I couldn't focus.

Teddy grabbed me by the shoulder and spun me around. He had tears streaming down his face as he hugged me hard. There was a small break in the firing, as both sides stood and watched in awe as the building had collapsed right in front of all of us. A cheer arose from Riley's men. Those of us that remained, just sat there, stunned. The respite was brief and soon Riley's men took up their charge with renewed energy, knowing that we had just suffered a heavy blow. Roy was yelling in my ear that his men were almost out of ammo as well.

"Push," was all I said.

"What?" Roy asked.

"Close on them," I answered.

"That's what I like to hear!" Liam roared as he emptied his rifle.

"Mack?" Teddy said, staring at me.

"You heard me. I'm done with this running shit. We're gonna kill all these mother fuckers, even if we have to do it with our bare hands," I said.

"Mack, seriously, we really need to…" I cut Roy off, "I said PUSH!" I stepped out of the garage, opening with a fresh clip in my

AK and slowly started walking toward Riley's men. Taking care to aim all of my shots. I was trying to take down as many as I could, because I had no intention of reloading my rifle.

Liam joined me quickly, a sinister smile plastered on his face. This is what he lived for. It was like I had just given him the best Christmas present ever. The rest followed as well, albeit more reluctantly than Liam. They were good men, all of them and trusted me. Hopefully, today wouldn't be the day that turned out to be a mistake. My rifle clicked empty and I dropped it to the side. I pulled both of my pistols out of my harness and opened up on the men directly in front of me. Roy and his boys concentrated more on the troops behind us, while we were focused on the ones out front, for the moment.

Riley's troops paused for a moment as we began our push. Only some of them were armed with rifles. Riley had set this up before we helped him take out the military so he, obviously, hadn't time to rearm his men with all the new goodies he had gotten. Some had pistols, but a lot had bats, tire irons or knives. A few of the men in the front of the line smiled as they saw us coming toward them.

"Yeah, I'm gonna enjoy this," Liam said as he dropped his rifle and pulled his chrome Desert Eagle. We were only a couple dozen feet apart now. Every pull of his trigger dropped another of Riley's men.

Suddenly, there was a roar behind me. I felt a smile form on my face as I glanced over my shoulder to see Tom, Teddy and the others charge forward, pistols drawn. They ran by me and Liam, laying waste to as many as they could before we were fully engaged. The smile grew as I heard Liam howl and threw his pistol to the side, diving into a small group of Riley's men.

I put the last two rounds from my Sig, directly into the face of a guy, who I think was trying to surrender to me. I flipped the pistol and clubbed the man next to him in the head, with the butt end of it. I could feel the heat from the barrel through my thick leather gloves. I dropped it and my second piece to pull out my knives. One was an old Ka-Bar marine knife, while the other was a Gerber Mark II.

The Ka-Bar slid silently into one man's abdomen. I punched him in the back of the head with my free hand as he doubled over, sending him smashing to the ground. I looked around to see that Liam had waded into the middle of the group. He had gotten a hold of a crowbar and was swinging away, creating a wide swath of bodies falling around him. They were trying to surge ahead to get inside the arc of his swing and I lost sight of him in a mass of bodies.

The sound of footsteps brought me back to my position as a guy charged at me with his knife, waving wildly above his head. I blocked his awkward down swing with my left and shoved my blade up under his ribs. I watched the life drain from his eyes as blood dribbled out from between his clenched teeth. Spinning free as his body dropped, I waded into the sea of writhing bodies. I walked up behind one man and shoved my Gerber up under the base of his skull. Pulling it free, I got smacked hard across the cheek with the butt of a pistol. I stumbled to the side and almost went down. I dropped the Gerber and caught myself with my left hand.

I looked up, just in time, to see the barrel of an old .45 swinging toward my face. I swung my right arm up, knocking the pistol to the side, as I stood. I caught him in the sternum with an open hand punch, with my left. He gasped as I knocked the wind out of him. Bringing my right back, I cut him deep across the cheek. Putting his left hand up to his face to hold it together, he swung a wild haymaker with his right. I ducked under it and he almost spun himself completely around. I popped up and helped him. Standing behind him I hooked my left arm up under his and grabbed the top of his head, yanking it back hard. I slid my blade across his throat, and only let his head go after I heard him start gurgling and choking on his own blood.

I saw Tom get smacked with the butt end of a rifle from behind as a second guy wound up with a crowbar to finish him off. He was less than ten feet away as I started shoving bodies trying to get to him. I yelled to try and get the guy with the crowbars attention, it didn't work. I threw an elbow at someone's head and yelled again as the blow started to fall. I heard a gunshot and saw the man's eyes go wide. I glanced to my right and saw Teddy holding a pistol in one hand and a blood covered aluminum baseball bat in the other. Tom's bald head popped up in the crowd, smiling I realized I had been holding my breath as I finally exhaled.

My joy was short lived. I had been paying too much attention to my men's well being and it almost cost me dearly. I got caught by a right hook. It felt like someone hit me with in the face with a rock. I went down hard and instantly felt boots pounding away at my ribs. I covered my face and felt at least one rib snap. I tried crawling deeper into the mass of bodies and that seemed to just encourage more of them to kick at me, trying to stomp me like a bug. I quickly flipped over onto my back and caught a heel in the face that may have broken my nose. The foot rose again and I caught it on its way down. Holding firmly to the sole of the boot I sat up. When I got up onto one knee, I had this guys leg jacked high in the air. His friends started pummeling on my back and head. I jammed the Ka-Bar deep into his inner thigh. He squealed as he tried to flail away from me. He pin wheeled, landing hard on his tailbone. Last I saw he was trying to hold his thigh shut as he was swarmed over by his buddies.

One of the men behind me hit me hard at the base of the skull, sending stars shooting across my field of vision. I staggered forward, trying desperately not to fall again. I didn't think my ribs would tolerate much more punishment. I spun, leading with my knife. He caught my hand and wrenched it until I dropped the blade. He was slightly taller than I was. The man was black with dreadlocks and an evil little smirk on his face. He was wearing an olive drab, military style vest, black cargo pants and black gloves. He pounded my face when he saw my hesitation at being stripped of my weapon. Over and over, he slammed away on the left side of my skull while still holding my hand in an iron grip.

I finally got my hand up high enough to block one of his shots. Quickly, he shoved my hand to the side and pulled back to start again. I stepped in close, swung my leg around his and fell into him. I'd like to say I threw myself into him, but I was so dazed by his punches, that I just sort of fell. He stumbled backwards then we both fell together. He let go of my right hand, so he could catch himself. Seizing the second of freedom, I grabbed him by the throat with it. We landed hard. He caught me in the ribs with a shot, knocking the wind out of me as I slammed my forehead into his nose. I heard a crack and a grunt. He pulled hard on my hand around his throat, my thumb dug in directly below his Adams apple. I fought off his attempts and got my second hand around it as well. I leaned forward and drove all my weight down on my hands. I could feel his fingers clawing at my wrists, biting deep through the skin. Teeth gritted, I dug my thumbs in harder, choking off any air from getting into his lungs. Eyes wide he flailed wildly. I pulled my knee up and held down one of his shoulders with it. He turned a dark purple and his body started to buck as it fought to survive. I growled and he almost threw me clear, but I shifted my weight and soon he stopped fighting. I held on for another twenty second, or so to make sure he was gone. It occurred to me, as I let go of the dead man's throat that it had gotten very quiet, almost calm. I knelt between his splayed legs and slowly glanced over my shoulder.

It seems the fight had wound down while I was preoccupied. Tom, Liam and the others stood behind me. The newer members of Alpha looked... shaken. I pushed myself to my feet, slowly, and stumbled forward as I walked toward them. Tom reached out and grabbed me by the shoulder. Guiding me over to a short wall, he nodded for me to sit down. I stared at him and returned the nod as I sat. "You okay?" Tom asked as he gave my face a quick exam.

"Aside from getting pummeled and a cracked rib or two I think I'm good," I answered. "Everyone else okay?"

"We lost a few, some bumps, bruises and cracked skulls, but otherwise yeah we're good," Teddy said, plopping down next to me.

"Yeah, I think the new bloods are kinda fucked up. I don't think they've had to do any up close killing before," Liam said hooking a thumb over his shoulder at the newer Alpha members. Woodsie looked a strange shade of green, Jim was a bit pale and Eric seemed to be not upset at all. For some reason, I found that interesting as I sat there catching my breath. Roy, Sampson and those that remained from Roy's team, joined us a minute or two later. By that point, I had retrieved my knives and guns as well as checked a few bodies for spare ammo. Tom explained that while I was occupied, a decent sized group had decided that they didn't feel like dying today and ran off.

"We should probably get moving then. I'm betting they come back soon and they'll more than likely bring friends," I said, pushing myself to my feet. The aching had started already from the beating I had taken and my left eye was pretty well swollen shut.

Sampson took point and led us to the safe house. It was a couple miles away in a straight line, but Sampson figured it would be better if we didn't lead Riley's men right to it in case someone was trailing us. A couple miles turned into at least three. My legs were jelly by the time we finally got to the building. A couple of his men saw us coming and made sure the main doors were open by the time we got there. It was a warehouse type building that was all boarded up. There were old office spaces in the front, which led to a wide open storage space in the back. I saw a couch in one of the offices and planted myself on it. I told Teddy to go find the others and bring them to me. He chuckled and muttered something about my age as he trotted off to find the others. I just groaned and waved him off weakly before I rolled over, trying to wish the aching away.

## Chapter 13

"OW!" I said as Chris sewed my head back together.

"Okay, so now what?" George asked. I had spent the last fifteen minutes, filling everyone in on what had happened outside the hospital and another ten getting Georges' report on how the evacuation went. It was a rather dismal conversation on both ends. We had just lost a lot more close friends and no one was in a good mood. Even though we were safe for the moment held up in one of the resistance's safe house.

"OW, JESUS!" I said again. It felt like Chris was stabbing me in the back of the head instead of stitching me up. "The only option I see is to go after the source and take Riley out," I said with a heavy sigh.

"We're running a bit low on men and supplies," George reminded me.

"I don't really need more men. It'll just be me and whatever members of Alpha that are willing to go. I won't sacrifice any more men for this lunatic," I said.

"Alright, we're gonna need intel from Sampson's people then, to figure out how to get in," George said, looking over to Sampson who had already been bandaged up. Sampson nodded in recognition.

"OW, honey, what the fuck?" I asked, spinning around to face Chris who was sitting on the back of the couch.

"Sorry," she growled.

"Uh oh," I heard Hags mutter.

"You okay?" George asked.

I saw her face go from somewhat composed, to angry, to upset and back to angry in the span of five seconds. "No, no I'm not okay at all," she said, hopping off the couch. "I'm not sure if any of you idiots noticed or not, but we came down here to get rid of the military and from what I can tell, we have. We've also managed to get a shitload of friends, family and strangers killed in the process. You'll have to forgive me for thinking that going back after this moron is an incredibly bad idea!" she said, planting her hands on her hips.

"Chris, honey you're just upset, we all are," Teddy said, stepping up to put a comforting hand on her shoulder. She promptly slapped it away.

"Teddy, I swear to God, if you try to calm this upset, little girl down, one more time, I will fucking shoot you in the foot, you condescending bastard!" she said, pulling her Sig out.

"Woah!" Teddy said, backing up until he was behind George.

"I have been to hell and back with you assholes for five years. I have always backed you and stitched you up when you needed me to. No more, we need to get the fuck out of here and go home. We did what we came to do and it's time to get the hell out of Dodge," she said, pacing the room and talking wildly with her hands.

"I know hon, but we can't just leave these people with him," I said, trying to get her to see my side.

"Why can't we? The way I see it, this is their problem. No offense Sampson, but you idiots are the ones who let him get this far. Someone shoulda killed him a long time ago. How is this, our mess to clean up?" she asked, glaring at me.

"None taken," Sampson said quietly, holding an ice pack to his head.

"We came down here to free this city, not leave it in a worse condition than we found it in," I said, trying to stand, feeling the dizziness, deciding against it, and sitting back down.

"What about leaving us in a worse condition? We've lost almost all of our men, and I dunno about the rest of you, but I am sick to death of watching what little family I have left die in this stinking city. I refuse to do this anymore. You are all just fucking crazy high on testosterone if any of you thinks sticking around is a good idea. Those of us with any sense at all, want to go home, NOW!" she said. I could have sworn she was going to stomp her feet and had to stare at the ground to keep from smiling.

"I didn't wanna say anything before Mack, but I have to say, I think she has a very valid point," George said.

"You didn't want to say anything?" I asked.

"You're in charge Mack, we follow you, not question," Teddy said, stepping out from behind his large friend.

"So, do you all agree with Chris?" I asked, looking around, trying to gauge every ones response.

"I do," Tom said.

"Kinda," Woodsie answered.

"Ayep," Hags said with is arms folded in the doorway. The rest of the room seemed to agree that it was time to go home as well.

135

"Hell Mack, even I agree. I mean, of course we could use the help, but you guys have taken a massive beating down here. I can't blame any of you for wanting to leave," Sampson said with a shrug.

I stared at my closest friends and family in disbelief. They looked like hell, each and every one of them. Battered, bruised and beaten. For the first time since we had formed our little group, they wanted to give up. I wanted to give up. I was tired like I never knew I could be. I hurt in places I didn't know were capable of pain. There was silence as I soaked it all in. A slight, almost imperceptible nod from the big man Sampson seemed to absolve me. The decision was made then and there. "Alright, if everyone is set on it, we'll go home," I said with a weak smile and a shrug. The mood instantly seemed to lighten and Chris even gave me a quick kiss before climbing back on the couch to finish sewing me up.

The news that we were going home seemed to reenergize everyone as well. There was a flurry of activity in the resistance warehouse. Sampson offered a couple of school buses to get us home since our convoy had, by now, been confiscated by Riley. Sampson saved the day yet again by making sure we had food, and spare gas for the trip home. It would only take four or five hours, once we got rolling. It took us forever to get down here because we had so many troops with us. That was no longer the case. We could fit everyone left, along with our meager supplies, on three school buses. That's down quite a bit from twenty five hundred men and dozens of vehicles.

Teddy had gone with Sampson and a few of his men to get the buses. They'd be stored here for a couple days, so we could get them all packed and fueled. We weren't leaving for another two days, so that we could catch our collective breath and hopefully heal up a bit. The roads hadn't been maintained for over five years. The ride down was rough enough, for the casualties we had going home with us, every bump would be agony.

Chris was so happy to be going home that she made sure to take that first night off. She claims to have wanted to spend some time thanking me. I myself, think she just wanted to have a normal night's sleep. It was the first time in ages that we had gotten anytime to be alone, well almost alone. Lily had made sure to curl up at the end of the bed roll once things had quieted down.

At first I didn't think that I'd want to do anything beside sleep the night away, because I ached all over. After a little bit of coaxing, Chris convinced me otherwise and I pushed through the pain, so to speak. I started to get a bit excited myself the next day. My injuries started to hurt less and I could almost open my left eye. Chris checked the stitches in my head and gave me an all clear thumbs up.

"How are things today?" Sampson asked, as I carried a box of food over next to one of the buses.

"Things are pretty okay actually," I answered, "How 'bout you?"

"I'm alright," he said with a small nod, "been getting reports that Riley's still looking for you, but he's nowhere near here."

"That's a bonus," I said, leaning against the side of the bus.

"Yeah, hopefully we can get you out before he starts looking up this way," he said. "Listen, I just wanted to thank you for all your help. I know you hate the idea of leaving, but your wife is right. You've all lost more than you ever should have. This is our fight. You got rid of the military. The rest should be up to us. If we can't take control of our own city from some… thug, then we don't really deserve it."

"No, you're right, we've lost so many and taken such a beating. To keep going after him for revenge would be more like suicide," I said, hanging my head, "It's time to go home. I've put enough people at risk already."

"Beside, you came down here expecting one fight, not two completely different ones. Consider me and my people as your relief column. You get to fall back for a bit and we'll keep the fight goin'," Sampson said with a small grin.

"You will get him right?" I asked, glancing at the big man.

"Yep, we will, and the day I do, I will send a runner, in my fastest car, to tell you that we did, you have my word," he said, holding out his hand.

"Thank you, that helps some," I said, shaking his hand.

He gave me a smile that said he knew I was lying and that it didn't really help at all. It was the best he could offer though and I'm glad he did. I believe him when he told me that he'd get Riley. I just didn't like the idea of someone else doing it. He had taken so many of my men that nothing short of killing him myself was going to make me feel better and Sampson understood that. *Now, if he offered to send Riley's head with the runner…*, was what I was thinking as I walked off to visit Drake.

They had set him up in one of the small office cubicles in the front of the building. It wasn't that he was special or anything, he just needed the most attention, since he was still laid up. I walked in to find him sitting up with pillows propped behind him. Sam was reclining in an old leather office chair. She was a petite girl and her pregnant belly seemed about ready to burst.

"Hey buddy," Drake said as I came in.

"Hey," I said, walking over to Sam and kissing her on top of the head before pulling up a chair.

"I'm the one who got shot, how come you're the one that looks like shit?" he asked with a chuckle. The laughing hurt his stomach. He winced and pressed on his wound.

"That's what ya get," I said, smirking.

"I hear we're going home soon?" Sam asked.

"Yep, buses are starting to get packed now," I answered with a smile.

"Thank God, I dunno how much longer I can hold this thing inside. I know I'd much rather deliver the baby at home than in a dirty bus on the road somewhere," she said, looking relieved.

I laughed softly. "Just hold on a couple more days then and we'll be home," I said.

There was an awkward silence as we all sat there. After almost a minute, Sam caved in and stood. "I'm gonna go see if Chris needs any help," she said with a fake smile and waddled out.

"Whew," Drake said, wiping his hand across his forehead, "I thought she'd never leave."

"I know huh?" I said.

"So, what's up? You look miserable. Is it because that prick Riley isn't dead yet?" Drake asked.

"It's like we share the same mind some days," I said, nodding.

"That'd be bad, some of the thought's I've had of you might make things a bit awkward," Drake said, grinning.

"Or awesome," I said, shaking my head.

"It's killin' you though, isn't it?" he asked.

"Yeah," I grumbled.

"I'm not happy about it either," he said.

"I figured," I said.

"So, are you gonna overturn this?" he asked.

I stood, pacing back and forth at the end of his bed. "I can't, neither of us are in any shape to take him and his men on."

"When has that ever stopped us?" he asked, being completely serious.

"Yeah, I know," I sighed.

There was a light knock on the door. "Excuse me," a soft voice said. I glanced over to see a pretty girl in her late twenties, with long brown hair and bright blue eyes standing in the doorway.

"Hello," I said casually.

"Mr. Mackenzie?" the girl asked.

"What's up?" I asked.

"Your wife asked me to come fetch you. It seems that Samantha's water has broken," she said with a small smile.

Drake bolted up in his bed and winced. "JESUS!" he exclaimed.

"Woah cowboy, you stay here," I said, putting a hand on his shoulder to keep him from jumping out of the bed altogether.

"But!" he said, looking as if he was about to panic.

"It's just her water. Let me go take a look and if she's close, I'll come and get you. No reason for you to get up, if she's gonna be in labor for another eight hours," I said, smiling.

"You promise you'll come get me?" he asked.

"Yep, I'll even make sure you get updated if it'll be a while," I said with a grin as I ducked out the door with the girl.

"What happened? Sam was just with us?" I asked as we walked.

"I'm not really sure. She came over to help your wife move supplies. Next thing I know, they're asking me to find you. I think the lifting combined with all the running and climbing caused her to go into labor is all Mr. Mackenzie," she said with a shrug.

"Just Mack is fine," I said with a smile.

"Just Mack it is then sir, I'm Charlotte by the way," she said, giving a little nod.

"Great to meet you Charlotte, I take it you got stuck here huh?" I asked as we turned the corner into a short hallway.

"Yep, I was here for a medical conference. After the meteor hit, there was mass rioting here in the city. I volunteered to help out at one of the hospitals and by the time things calmed down, there was no way to get home," she said sadly.

"Sorry to hear that. Where was home?" I asked as we turned into a small room.

"Manchester England," she said. "I found him Christina. He was right where ya said he'd be."

Christina was standing next to Sam who was lying on a leather couch. There was a white sheet covering her from the waist down and her legs were bent at the knee. "Thank you Charlotte," Chris said.

"Looks like someone couldn't wait for us to get home huh?" I asked.

"I tried Mack," Sam said, looking flushed.

"You did great hon, everything's gonna be fine," I said leaning down and kissing her on the forehead.

"Charlotte here is one of the local doctors. Sampson says she helps with a lot of the deliveries," Chris said, trying to reassure Sam.

"How hard can it be, you girls have been doing it for a few thousand years," Drake said from behind me. His face was ashen.

"You were supposed to stay in bed," I said.

"Yeah, get me a chair would ya? My gut hurts," he said as he staggered by me to stand next to Sam.

I chuckled and shook my head as I grabbed a metal folding chair from the other side of the room. Drake dropped into it almost before I had it open. He was pale and in pain, but there was no way he was missing the birth of his kid. Well, unless he passed out.

"Is it here yet?" I heard from the doorway. I looked over my shoulder to find Teddy, Roy and George, hovering expectantly in the doorway.

"No, her water just broke like five minutes ago," Chris said.

"Hey, I was out lickety split after my mother's water broke," George said.

"Well, at least you made your mom happy once in your life," Teddy said, nodding slowly.

"True, I was a pretty horrible kid," George said.

"Pretty horrible adult too," Teddy said, smirking.

"Saw that one coming," Roy said.

"Will you three get out of here for a little bit please?" Chris asked.

"Sure, Sure," George answered.

"Take him too," Chris said, pointing to me.

"Okay, okay, I'm going," I said, throwing my hands up in the air, feigning indignation. As we walked down the short hallway, we heard Sam grunt and cry out as a contraction came rolling through.

"We're not going too far. I'm betting this will be quicker than we think," I said to George.

"I'll go find us some chairs," Teddy said, jogging off.

"Thanks," I said, leaning against the wall.

"Is this gonna delay us?" George asked.

"Maybe by a day or so, shouldn't be too bad as long as there isn't any complications," I shrugged. "It's just a bus ride,"

"I'm gonna hope there's no complications either way. They deserve a little happiness," George said.

"Amen brotha," I mumbled.

I saw Teddy coming toward us carrying some folding chairs. Lily quickly sauntered by him, stopping to tilt her head at me for a moment, before making her way down the hallway and turning into the room where Chris and Sam were. "**LILY!**" I heard Chris yell a second or two before Lily came quickly back out. She made a small circle and curled up in the doorway to keep an eye on things. I chuckled softly as she grunted. She seemed annoyed that she had been tossed out.

"Everything okay?" I asked loudly.

"Yeah, she just kept sticking her nose everywhere trying to figure out what the hell was going on is all," Chris answered.

"Well in her defense, I'm betting it probably is an odd set of smells," I said with a smirk. I popped open the chair and plunked myself down in it, leaning the metal back against the wall and lifting the front legs in the air.

"I don't have her nose and it's an odd set of smells!" Chris exclaimed.

"**CHRISTINA!**" I heard Sam yell.

"Sorry hon, it's completely natural," she said, apologizing. I could hear Drake snickering for a moment before Sam told him to shut up or leave.

Within a couple minutes, both Anne and Liam had joined us in the hallway. Liam sat Indian style against the wall, while Anne paced nervously up and down the hallway. Occasionally poking her head into the delivery room to see how things were going.

"You know you could just ask from the hallway," I said as she paced by me.

"What if something goes wrong though?" she asked, chewing on a nail.

"We're five feet away. There isn't even a door between us. I can already hear much more than I'm usually comfortable with," I said with a grimace.

"I wanna be there though for the birth," she said, furrowing her brow at me.

"You are here for the birth. If you got any closer, you'd be in there with the kid," Teddy said.

"I mean, I wanna see it," she said, hands on her hips.

"Then grab a chair and go in to sit with Drake hon, your pacing is making everyone else testy," Liam said.

"Hmmph," she grumbled and ducked inside.

"Thanks," George said. Liam nodded in return.

Charlotte came in and out a couple times in the next half hour. Every time she came out she was smiling, assuring us that everything was fine. She would toddle off to grab more towels or to find another person to fetch her some hot water. I myself was a big fan of pretty girls with British accents, so I could have listened to her give orders all day. From what I could tell from the smiles on the other guys faces, they felt the same way.

Under an hour later, we heard grunting and screaming, followed by a short silence, then a small cry. There was a mad rush to get into the doorway. I'm not too proud to say that there was a fair amount of shoving and a couple elbows tossed as well. I saw Drake once I got inside, he was sitting, holding a bundle of blankets. He had the most serene and happy smile on his face that I had ever seen. He glanced up at me, pulled the edge of the blanket back and introduced me to his daughter, "Say hello to your uncle Mack, he doesn't always look quite this scary, but he's having a bad week."

"Not anymore I'm not. As of today, this might be the best week I've had in a long time," I said softly as I brushed her tiny cheek with my rough calloused fingertip, while drinking in every bit of her beauty and innocence. "She's gorgeous," I said quietly, leaning down to kiss her wrinkled nose. I gave Drakes shoulder a squeeze as I stepped behind him and over to Chris and Sam. I wanted to let the others ogle and bask in the new baby's joy.

"Actually, she looks like an alien," Drake said.

"True, but she's one gorgeous alien. Now shut up," I said.

Amidst the ooing and ahhing, someone asked if they had a name picked out. Sam then announced that this beautiful little girls name was Megan, after Sam's mother. Drake sat holding her, singing to her softly, ignoring everyone else in the room. Within a few minutes, Charlotte started to herd people out of the room. Sam was tired from the delivery and Charlotte wanted her to get some rest. Once everyone had shuffled out into the hall, she closed the door, so that Sam and Drake could get some rest.

Sampson found me a little while later all smiles and sunshine. "I take it you've heard about the baby," I said, grinning.

"I did, congrats on the new addition," he said with a firm handshake.

"I'll pass that on to Drake and Sam, they did all the work," I said.

"Make sure that you do. Pass one of these along as well," he said as he handed me two plastic cigar tubes.

I glanced down at the plastic tubes and smiled to myself. "Fuente's huh? Very nice, you sure you don't wanna hang onto these?" I asked.

"Nah, I've never smoked a day in my life. I found a couple boxes ages ago. I keep them for this very purpose actually," he said with a shrug.

"Excellent and thanks, I'm sure Drake will enjoy this immensely. Just as soon as we can pry the baby out of his arms," I chuckled as I slid the tubes into my shirt pocket.

"Good, good, are you guys gonna need a couple of extra days before you head home?" he asked.

"I'm gonna check with Charlotte and Chris to see what they think before I push our timetable back," I answered, as he nodded in agreement.

"There's plenty of room, so it's fine if you do," he said.

"Thanks, for everything," I said with a smile.

"You're welcome," he said, "I've been thinking about how to get you out of here safely."

"You too huh?" I asked. "I know they're all excited about going home, but I don't think they remembered that we need to get by the big guns at the edge of town, before we can go anywhere."

"That's why you're in charge. You think of that shit," Sampson said with a grin.

"So that's the reason huh? Unfortunately, I think my people are too beat up for that fight," I shrugged.

"I was thinking about that as well. I think you're right there as too. Your people aren't in any shape for another battle, even one as small as that would be," he agreed.

"I hate to ask…" I started to say before he cut me off, waving a hand for me to stop. "I've already thought of this, we should have no problem taking out one detachment of men and a couple cannons. It's the least we can do to help," he said.

"Thank you, again," I said.

"No problem at all. I would like to go over the plan with you, if that's ok. You do have a bit more experience in this area," he said. "Let me know later, what the doctors say about Sam traveling and we'll figure things out from there," he said with a wink.

"Will do," I said with a nod, before I turned to go check in with Chris.

Both Chris and Charlotte agreed that it would be better if we could push the timetable back twenty four hours. There was nothing wrong with Sam or the baby, but it'd give Sam a chance to recover a bit and have a more comfortable ride home. We all wanted to get home as quickly as possible, but I saw no reason to make Sam miserable. I could tell Chris hated the idea of waiting another day, but she knew it'd be more helpful if we did.

It was fine with me. It'd give me more time to throw together a plan, now that I knew Sampson would be helping us out. I wandered off to find George, Hags and the others, to let them know we'd be staying a little longer and that I needed them later to help me and Sampson figure out how to get us a clear road home. I wasn't quite sure how well that was gonna work out. Guess I'd just have to have a bit of faith in Sampson and his men.

## Chapter 14

We were finally ready to go home. Plans had been made, routes had been mapped out. The buses had been packed with supplies. Everyone was excited to be heading out. Most were looking forward to leaving New York far behind us. The city had kicked our asses and left a nasty taste in our mouths.

There was electricity in the resistance storehouse the morning of our departure. It felt like when I was back in school, getting ready to go on the big class field trip. People were running around, finishing up last minute preparations and saying goodbye to new friends that we had made the last few days.

I was sitting off in a corner talking to Sampson and Hags. We had gone over the plan over a dozen times in the last couple days, but I still felt that it needed to be gone over one last time. I didn't like the idea of waiting until the last minute to clear the road ahead of us, but Hags and Sampson were right in the fact that if we cleared it too early, we'd just be tipping Riley off so he could reinforce the area with more men... then we'd be screwed.

Riley's men had been scouring the city looking for us the last few days. I knew they'd still be out there. At this point, I was just hoping to not run into any on our way out of town. Sampson was checking his gear as he talked to us. He made sure his radio and ear bud worked fine one last time before he and his men left. They were getting a one hour head start. We walked him over to the trucks, where his men were waiting. It was early, and the sun was nowhere near coming up. If everything worked out, it would be getting light when we were about thirty miles into Connecticut.

"Thanks again for the help," Hags said as Sampson hopped into the passenger seat of a black van.

"It's the least we can do for you," he said, as the two men shook hands. "It was really good to see you again Mack, maybe next time we can do it without all the bullets."

"Wouldn't that be a nice change," I said, scratching at the stitches in my head.

"We'll be in touch with the radios and I'm sure I'll say it again but, take care and have a safe trip home," Sampson said with a smile

145

before he closed the door to the van. It slowly rolled off into the black of the night. We had set up diversionary attacks at two other locations. That way, even if Riley could send men, he wouldn't know which location to send them to.

Hags and I watched the last of his vehicles get outside the warehouse before we turned back toward our buses. I could hear the heavy corrugated doors ratcheting shut behind us. It was time for us to start getting ready to leave as well. George got the team leaders together to go over our final check list. Each of them was in charge of something having to do with our preparations.

Once that was taken care of, we started loading everyone onto the buses. Doctors, nurses and wounded, along with Teddy and his team, were going on one bus. That one would be driven by George. The other two were going to be filled with men and supplies. Me and Alpha would be on the middle bus along with Roy's team and Hags would be in the last bus with two of the other teams. I checked in with Sampson and the other two teams. They were just getting into position. It had only taken forty minutes. He told me they'd be ready to go in under five minutes. I wished him happy hunting and took a deep breath before I got back to work. Rounding everyone up and onto the buses didn't take long at all. Getting an accurate head count was a bit more difficult.

In the end, we had a whopping two hundred and seventeen people traveling home, including our newest member Megan. As well as one dog. We came down with over ten times that many. There was a massive lump in my throat when I heard the final tally. We had lost so many friends and family, and we couldn't even bring their bodies home for a decent burial. After doing a final check of all three buses, I climbed the rubberized steps of the middle bus and heard the pneumatic doors hiss as they shut behind me.

Chris had decided to ride with me, since all of our wounded were mobile and stable. There was really no need for her to be up in the first bus with them. I radioed to the other buses and watched as the first bus rolled out through the corrugated steel doorway. I always loved long road trips, but the giant ball of worry that I had in my gut, as we drove out onto the main road, wasn't going to get any better until we were well out of the city.

The bus was quiet and tense. Everyone knew that this was our one chance to get out safely. I was checking in with the other two buses every few blocks. It would take us about thirty minutes to reach the edge of the city, if all went well. The buses rumbled along on the dark streets of the city, the combination of neglected roads and worn out old shocks made for one hell of a bumpy ride.

I was sitting next to Chris, staring out the grimy front window of the bus. Looking for any sign that something was wrong. I felt her hand on my thigh and glanced over to see her smiling up at me. She could tell I was worried. "It'll be okay hon," she said before she laid her head on my shoulder.

"I know," I replied, as I kissed the top of her head. I didn't actually believe it, but it felt like the right thing to say.

Another few blocks and I checked in again with the others. Everything seemed quiet and I started to think maybe I was worrying about nothing. Sampson was a trained soldier in command of other trained men. The small detachment at the border shouldn't be a problem for them. I hadn't heard from him yet and that was unsettling. It should have been a very quick engagement, no longer than ten to fifteen minutes, at most. I glanced down at my watch and felt a lump in my throat, almost thirty minutes had passed since I'd heard from him.

I keyed the radio and waited. No response, I stood and paced toward the front of the bus, keying the mic again. It took almost a minute, but I finally heard static and a voice. "Lil busy here Mack. There was a much larger force than we thought. We're almost through though, you should be good to go when you get here," Sampson said. I could hear rifle fire behind him.

"Copy that, we are on schedule so far. We should be there in about fifteen," I said, dropping back into the seat next to Chris.

I felt my heart starting to beat faster. I had to close my eyes for a minute and focus my breathing. It felt like the beginning of a panic attack, but not as all encompassing. It was the feeling I got, when I knew something was going to go wrong. It was just a gut instinct I had always had, even as a child. I didn't consider it anything overly special, but it had served me well over the years. Every fiber of my being wanted to turn around and get back to the warehouse.

I looked around the bus and everyone else seemed calm, almost serene. I could even hear some of them joking further back. My pulse pounded in my ears and I could feel the pit of my stomach trying to climb up my throat. I could call the abort at any time, but what then? We needed to get out and get out now. If we turned back, all of

Sampson's work would be for nothing and Riley would have all the time he needed to track us down. At that point, we'd all be dead, Sampson and his people included.

I screwed my eyes shut, trying to get rid of the voices in my head screaming to give the abort call, when I heard an actual voice in my ear. "Mack I have movement back here," I heard Hags say.

"You what?" I almost yelled.

"Your guys say they see movement. At least one car, but since they're runnin' without lights they can't be sure," he answered.

"**FUCK!**" was all I could think to say. I was up in a flash, and called to the front bus to fill them in. I stood next to our driver so he'd hear as well.

"Should we open up?" I heard Buck in my ear. His team was on the third bus with Hags.

"Umm, yeah let's see if we can discourage them from getting any closer. Take them out if you can. I'm sure they've already been on the horn to Riley though," I said, pacing the length of the bus.

"Copy that, kickin' the door now," I heard my friend say. I didn't need the radio to hear the M-60 he turned loose on the front end of the car. I could hear it chugging away, just fine, without the earpiece.

I squeezed my temples and shook my head, trying to think. "No one stops," I said so that everyone could hear me. "Is everyone clear? If you see something happen to one of the other buses, you keep fucking going." I was calm now. This was business mode for me. I always hated not knowing what was going to go wrong. Once I knew though, I was good and all worry was banished from my brain. You either got your ass out of the fire or you burned, either way it was simple. The complexity came when you had no idea what, where, or how big the fire was going to be.

"But Mack…" I head George say. I cut him off knowing that the dissention would come from him, of course. "It wasn't a request George. We can't win this fight. If I could split us all up to different routes, I would. That option is off the table now, so you just run hard and fast and get as far the fuck away as you can. You especially George, you have the docs, wounded and Megan. There's no way you fend off a concentrated attack, or helps one of us to do it. We'll do what we can back here, but no one stops. This is our one shot to get out," I said. When I finished I sat down and checked my magazines.

"Fuck you Mack, we're a team!" I heard Drake yell in my ear.

"Not today we're not buddy. I need you to make sure he does what he's told. Your little girl and the docs need to be safe," I said calmly.

"NO!" Drake sputtered.

"Listen, we have no idea what's going to happen yet, but those are your orders and how about for a fuckin' change, you do as you're fuckin' told!," I growled.

I waited for a couple seconds to get a reply and when none seemed to be coming, I continued, "I have no intentions of leaving anyone behind, but if we all stop, then a lot more people are going to die. I don't see it happening. Those are the standing orders in case it does. If we get separated somehow then we all meet up at Larchmont and figure it out from there agreed?"

I got an affirmative from all three drivers, Drake and Hags. "Mack, the first car is down, but I'm pretty sure we have multiple contacts back there behind it. Nobody has returned fire yet, but they are closing in," Buck said from the third bus.

"Copy that, get me numbers when you can, and if you can make out a target, feel free to waste as much ammo as you see fit," I said.

"Copy that sir," he replied. "George, pick it up a bit, you're on point up there," I said.

"I'll try, but this bus is almost rattling apart at the seams at this speed," he answered.

"I don't care if we leave pieces of her from here to the edge of town, pick it up," I said.

'I'm on it," he said.

I keyed the mic on the radio and hoped Sampson had some good news for me. "How we lookin' Sampson?" I asked.

"We're getting there Mack, how're things on your end?" he asked.

"Shitty actually," I said.

"You still moving?" he asked.

"Yeah, we're movin'" I said.

"Copy that, just keep comin'," he said. That's when I heard the cannons. **BOOM, BOOM, BOOM** thundered from the distance. We were still a few miles away, but we could hear them clear as day. "Aw fuck," I heard Sampson say. He sounded calm, but sincerely unhappy.

"Please tell me those aren't turned on you," I asked, knowing how close he was to them.

"Nope, outgoing, are they just firing blind?" he asked.

"Probably not," I said.

"How would they know where you are?" he asked, sounding stressed.

"Could be the multiple contacts behind us," I said with a heavy sigh.

"**OH FOR FUCK'S SAKE!** You may have wanted to mention that," he yelled.

"Why? What're you gonna do? You're a tad busy right now. Just shut those fuckin' cannons down. You don't worry about us," I said.

"Copy that," Sampson said, sounding pissed.

"George, I know you heard those. I need eyes up front to see how accurate they are," I said.

"Copy that, I didn't see where they landed," he said.

"Maybe they don't know how to aim them well," Chris said next to me. "It's not like they've had a lot of time to learn."

"Let's hope your right," I said.

I heard an explosion from the back it wasn't loud enough to be one of the cannons. "One more down Mack, unfortunately, they've turned on their lights and have started to return fire," Buck said.

I ran to the back of the bus and took a peek. I could see at least two other vehicles, one was a van or a truck, but that was all I could make out in the dark. The two had slid up next to the third bus and was peppering the side of it with rounds. Some of the men had jammed their weapons out the half open windows and were firing back. "Slide us to the left, so we can get some fire on those vehicles," I called out to the driver as I made my way to the emergency door in the back. The bus veered to the left and I kicked the metal bar forcing the door open. It swung wide and I opened up with my AK, riddling the front end of the van and taking out one of the headlights. I felt someone grabbing at my harness and spun my head to see Eric. "Just makin' sure you don't fall out the back boss," he said with a grin.

"Gonna get loud boss," Jim said as he opened up over my shoulder, while I changed magazines. He shattered the front windshield of the van with rounds from his M-16. It veered and swerved, but stayed alongside the third bus.

The car behind swung around the van and I could hear its engine roar as it passed it, trying to get to us.

"Excuse me guys." I heard from behind me. I glanced over my shoulder, to see Woodsie towering over us with his M-60 and a smile.

"Mind if I cut in?" he asked. The three of us moved, as quickly as we could, to let the big man through. Jim stepped in behind him, grabbing a hold of the webbing on Woodsie's harness to make sure he stayed in the bus, seconds before he opened up. The front end of the car exploded, almost instantly, as the larger rounds found the engine block of the old vehicle. It swerved, hitting the van. It blew out one of the larger vehicle's tires, before it flew off the side of the road and smashed into the front of a building.

I had moved toward the front of the bus, when I heard the cannons fire again, **BOOM, BOOM, BOOM**, off in the distance. "George let's see if we can pinpoint those rounds," I said.

"Copy…" There was a loud whistle and the front of George's bus exploded. The flash was blinding and I had to blink quickly. They had been a hundred yards ahead of us. The round struck, driving the front end of the bus into the ground. At the speed it was traveling it caused the ass end of the bus to jump straight into the air a good eight feet. The momentum kicked the back end out to the left and suddenly, there was a flaming ball, dancing sideways across the street, directly in our path. "**NOOOOO!**" I heard myself scream. It was almost drowned out by the yells from everyone else on the bus.

The second round landed behind us destroying Riley's vehicle and caused the others to pile up behind it. I winced as it landed, praying it wasn't going to fall on my head. I heard the driver of our bus screaming that we didn't have enough room to get out of the way of George's fireball that was getting closer every second. It had flipped once already and was starting to roll, as it left a trail of burning debris.

The third round landed not ten feet in front of us, kicking up dirt and debris, sending hot shrapnel flying in every direction. I dove to the floor of the bus. The driver had no such luxury. There was a quick scream as the windshield shattered and then just the roar of the wind. I screamed, "**HOLD ON!**" as I scrambled across the floor, trying to get back to Chris and the others. The bus started to swerve and veer now that it was driverless. I glanced up and saw Liam leaning across the back of Chris' seat. His arm stretched as he reached for me. I kicked hard and pushed off the floor. His leather gloved hand wrapped around my wrist as I locked mine around his meaty forearm. The world stopped, literally. Our bus slammed into the fiery wreck of George's bus and all forward motion seemed to cease instantly. I heard screams and a massive roar. People flew out of their seats and windows smashed.

Liam had wedged himself between his seat and the back of Chris'. Gravity ceased to exists for a moment as I felt my feet stay up in the air as he tried to reel me in like a fish on a line. Jim flew by me. Flailing, as he tried to find purchase on one of the leather seats. He landed hard and slid, I heard a crunch as he ran head first into metal pole at the top of the steps, near the front of the bus.

Woodsie plowed into me, something hit me hard in the ribs and I felt them crack. I could hear Liam bellowing as we yanked him over the top of the seat. The bus had bounced and there was a terrible screech of metal on metal as we jumped and rolled along, over, next to, and on top of the other bus in front of us. The chaos reigned as I fought to catch site of Chris, or even Lily. I got slammed off of every surface of the flipping bus. I still had a hold on Liam and my back slammed into the ceiling, driving the breath from my lungs. I saw blood on Liam's face and head, a lot of it. He had hit something hard. He bared his teeth one last time and pulled me toward him as we were flung around the cabin. He held me, pinned against his chest, with one arm as we fell again. I heard a crack next to my head as his other arm snapped in two trying to break our fall.

I came to choking and coughing. I couldn't seem to draw enough air to breathe. Everything was black and I felt like I was being crushed. Compared to the noise before I passed out, it was deathly silent. So much so, that I wondered if I had gone deaf. Panic set in quick and I started to squirm. My eyes took only a moment to adjust and I could see Liam's face. His eyes were open and he was covered in blood. I screamed and tried to shove him off of me. He was pinned on top of me by something else and I had to wriggle my way out from beneath the huge man. I pulled off my glove and pressed my fingers against his thick neck. I tried three different times, but didn't find a pulse.

I started to push myself up onto my knees and screamed again as I heard something grinding in my side. I looked around quickly. I was in the middle of the bus still, lying on the ceiling. The bus had flipped and come to rest on its roof. I couldn't see all the way to the front, which looked as if it had been melded into part of the first bus. There was smoke everywhere and fire only a few feet away, closer to the front end of the bus. Flipping onto my back, I looked around as best I could. I still had no sign of Chris, Lily, or even Anne.

I couldn't hear anything except the ringing in my ears and the crackle of the burning fire. The stench of the smoke made me cough and gag again. I shifted around and tried to crawl my way to where I had been sitting. There were bodies strewn all over the cabin, none seemed to be moving as I had to crawl over some people to get further back. I caught a glimpse of what looked like it could be blond hair and I scurried toward it as fast as I could.

I flung boxes and equipment aside, trying to reach what I thought might be Chris' blond hair. I had to pull someone from on top of her as well. I heard a small whining as I moved the second body and looked down. She was face down. I was on my knees and pulled her toward me as I sat back, yanking her into my lap. "C'mon honey I got ya, I got ya," I said as I brushed back her hair from her face. She had a huge gash on her forehead and I checked her neck for a pulse. "NONONONONO," I said over and over. Her face was serene and cold. I looked her up and down for injuries. Her leg was shot out at an odd angle, obviously broken. I moved my arm out from under her head to check the side of her body that was facing away from me and her head flopped down unnaturally. I stared at her for what seemed like forever. Her neck had been snapped cleanly. Suddenly, I couldn't breathe. I pulled her tight to my chest quickly as the tears came streaming down my bloody face. I heard the whining again and saw movement. Glancing up through the blur of tears, I saw that it was Lily, she was alive!

She crawled toward her mom and I, dragging herself by her front legs, until she got to where she could lay her head in my lap. She snuffled Chris' neck and lapped at her face, trying to wake her. I rubbed the top of Lily's head and for a moment, I was hopeful that she would be okay. That was quickly extinguished when I glanced down past the top of her neck. Her back legs weren't moving and I saw blood. I went to touch her fur in the area with the blood. She snapped and flinched in pain. I moved again to check, slower this time, and instantly burst back into tears as I saw that her spine was snapped in half. The back end had broken through the skin. There was massive bleeding and internal damage. Thankfully, it was snapped in twom so I was hoping that she wasn't in too much pain. "I'm so sorry, oh God I'm so sorry. I only wanted to keep you safe. Oh God why, why, why, why? Fuck why didn't we just stay the fuck home? Oh God I'm so sorry. Please Jesus, please, please, please, just stop this please fuuuuuuck."

I gently lifted Chris and moved her next to me, "I'll be right back baby, I just have to take care of something," I said softly as I kissed her forehead.

Stroking the side of Lily's face, I eased myself down next to her, so she could slather my face in kisses. I could hear her gasping for breath and figured at least one of her lungs had collapsed. Blood was dribbling from her mouth, but she kept trying to edge closer to me as if she wanted me to hold her. I brushed back her ears and stroked her down the top of her shoulders as I stared into her giant brown eyes. We had raised her from eight weeks old and she had been our pet, best friend, and loyal protector. She was as close to Chris and I as any child could be and I loved her so very much. She was trembling as she pawed at my hand and held it down to clean it.

I undid the snap on my harness and pulled my Sig from its' holster. I laid it in my lap and held Lily close. She was suffering so very much and through all that, she still just wanted to be with Chris and I, so that she could try and take care of us. I was crying so hard I was shaking. I could barely breathe, but still the tears came in choking sobs. I stroked her face again and smiled as I gazed for the last time into my beautiful Lily's big, dark brown eyes. I kissed her face and the fur on her neck as I slid the gun up to the side of her head. "I'm so, so sorry beautiful. I love you so much baby," I said, a second before I pulled the trigger, so that she wouldn't hurt any more.

The tears were still flowing as I moved Lily. I laid her gently next to her mom. I placed her, so that her head was on Chris' still chest. I kissed my wife one last time and crawled toward the side of the bus. I shoved myself through a small window, barely noticing that I must have cut myself in a half a dozen places as I exited the bus. I reached back in and grabbed my AK. Lying on the hard asphalt of the street, it took me about ten minutes to catch my breath. I rolled onto my stomach and forced myself up onto my knees. Stars flashed before my eyes as pain seared through my ribs and back. Finally, I stood, holding myself steady against the side of the bus. I looked to Georges' bus hoping to see some movement, but there was nothing, just flame. The whole bus had been burning for a good long time. The heat from it made my face hot. There had been spare gas cans on every bus. The ones on the first bus had gone up when they had been hit by the shell.

There wasn't much left of it even now. There was a dense cloud of smoke and silence except for the crackling of the fires. I walked around the wreckage of the two buses, straining my eyes in the dark for any kind of movement at all.

I stood staring blankly, for God knows how long. Every inch of my body begged me to just lie down and wait for the inevitable. I shook my head and started to limp along the road back toward the city. Where was the third bus? I tilted my head in confusion and glanced around. Spinning in a tight circle, I looked again. The third bus wasn't here. It hadn't wrecked. I saw a couple of Riley's cars that we had taken out as well as a couple more that looked like they wrecked when we did, but no third bus. "Huh, good for them," I said to no one at all.

I wished them well and figured if they had gotten past the cannons they should be in Larchmont already, waiting for any of us to show up. *Too bad none of us will*, I thought to myself as I limped toward one of Riley's vehicles.

The windshield had been shot out, but it looked otherwise intact. I pulled the driver's side door open. There was a groan and a cough. I looked inside and saw a pair of Riley's men. The passenger was dead, his skull caved in by hitting the windshield. The driver was the one making the noise. His face was bloody and he had his right hand pressed against his left side. He looked up at me, his eyes in pain, "Help a brotha out?" he said before he gave a sickening little chuckle, that instantly, turned into a gurgling cough.

I shuffled around the front end of the car. The headlights were still on, cutting sharply through the thick cloud of smoke. I pulled the passenger door open and yanked the body out. "Hey man, he's long dead seriously, help me out over here," he said, grabbing the wheel. The body thudded unceremoniously onto the ground. Stepping over it, I shut the passenger door as I walked back across the front. I could hear the driver cursing as I shambled back to his side. "Listen man; just help me out of here. I'm pretty sure I broke all my ribs on the steering column," he said, pleading with me.

I looked him up and down and nodded. From what I could tell, he had at least one broken leg as well, but I didn't think he needed to know that. I grabbed him by the collar of his coat and pulled hard. He screamed for me to stop, **"I'M STUCK, WAIT STOP, I'M STUCK I SAID,"** he yelled as I kept pulling. Finally, whatever it was he was stuck on gave way and he tumbled out of the driver's seat still screaming. He crawled a couple feet and threw himself onto his back, gasping for air and coughing up blood. He looked up at me nodding, "Thanks man," he said. I just stared at him as I pulled my Sig from its' holster and aimed it at his head. I pulled the trigger twice before he had a chance to protest. Sliding the gun back into the harness I slid behind the wheel. It took a few tries, but the engine finally turned over and sputtered to life. It didn't sound like it'd run for very long. I didn't need it to get me too far, just back to Grand Central.

## Chapter 15

The car smashed through the steel reinforced, glass doors at the front of Grand Central Station. My eyes had been closed as I hit, my head smashed into the steering wheel, breaking my nose I'm sure. I reached over and grabbed my AK from the passenger seat. I pulled the handle, and used the door frame to steady myself as I stood. My nose felt like it was full of cotton balls and I could swear that I could hear my ribs grinding.

I took a moment to assess how bad off I was. Broken nose and ribs made breathing a lot of fun. I was pretty sure the stitches in the back of my head had reopened from the bus accident. My ear felt wet and my hand came away red after touching it. Not sure how much of it was gone, but a chunk was definitely missing. There was a stabbing pain that shot down my right leg with every step. Either something was fractured, or I had a piece of shrapnel buried in there. I could feel a gash in my right side as well, but had no idea how bad it was at the moment and didn't really care. I closed my left hand around the wooden grip of the AK and winced at the pain. It felt like a couple of fingers and, maybe the hand itself, was broken.

I stared blankly around the huge station, lost in thought for just a moment. The guards from outside had regained their wits and came at me. One grabbed my right arm while the second went for the left. I came back to the moment as the second began pulling me toward him. Glancing to my left, I yanked my arm up at the same time as I slid my leg behind his. I shoved my elbow up under his chin and threw him off balance. He started to fall and I let myself drop with him. I heard a sickening crunch as my bony elbow crushed his windpipe. I rolled across him, up onto one knee and put three rounds into the other door guard. I could hear more men running up the granite stairs toward me. Standing to meet them, I saw three in front who tried to get out of the way. They hesitated for a fraction of a second too long. Firing from the hip, I hosed down the stairway with bullets. Some of the men in the back dove over the railings to avoid the hail of rounds.

There was a groan next to me. One of the three had pulled himself to the top of the stairs and had his face resting on the cool stone, next to my foot. I flipped the rifle around so that I had the barrel in my hand. His head turned slightly and tried to look up at me as I brought the heavy wooden stock down hard. After I hit it the third time it cracked and the groaning stopped as I stared at him.

"**RILEY**," I bellowed as I hobbled down the stairs.

"**RIIIILEEEYY**," I yelled again, dropping the AK and drew one of my Sigs. One of the men that had hopped the railing, popped out from my right. He took maybe a step from behind his cover before I put two slugs in his chest. I slid the gun quickly back in its holster and grabbed the railing to steady myself.

I heard clapping and spun to my left. My leg buckled a bit, but I caught it in time. I coughed hard and could taste blood in my mouth as I spit. "You look like shit Mack," Stacey said as she walked slowly toward me.

"Fuck you; get me Riley," I said, leaning against the railing.

"You know I can't do that," she said as she came closer, a blade in each hand.

"Oh, so you think you're gonna kill me to keep your cunt of a boss safe?" I spat as pulled both of my blades.

"I am an assassin Mack. It kinda goes with the title," she said, taking on a crouch, like the moment before a big cat pounces.

"Yeah, I forgot you're the tough chick," I said as I forced a chuckle, that shot pain through my ribs making me wince.

"You're damn right I am," she said with a smirk as she leaned in and took a quick swipe at me. Her technique was sloppy and she still managed to graze my side.

I reached out and punched her in the face. The blade of my knife tucked up against my forearm. Her face went from cocky to shocked in a millisecond. "Stupid bitch, you forgot that I have a longer reach than you do," I said a split second before I punched her a second time.

She roared and lunged at me. I dodged to the side, one of her blades cut the front of my thigh as she passed. I drove my fist into the back of her skull, shoving her face into the cold stone. She grunted as I wrapped my hand up in her ponytail. I yanked hard, with my knee buried in the small of her back. I'll give her credit; she gritted her teeth and took it as I nearly snapped her spine. "Still feel tough?" I asked. I heard her try and give me some smart ass answer, but it got cut off as I pounded her face into the smooth stone floor. Her front teeth and nose broke. She made a whimpering noise as I bashed her face a couple more times before pulling her up off the floor.

She was mostly limp and wouldn't have been able to stand if I hadn't been holding her by the front of her leather coat. I was gasping at the exertion and everything started to swim in front of me as I pulled her up. Her head hung, I cupped it in my left hand and lifted it so she could look at me. "Assassin huh?" I asked, shaking my head.

"Fuck you douchebag," she spat at me. Her next movement was predictable. She brought her arm up trying to jam her blade up under my ribs. I let go of her chin and swung my arm down, easily blocking the upward thrust of her dagger.

I smiled a little as I heard her knife go clanging across the floor. "You're just a sad, sad little girl," I stroked her cheek softly with my gloved hand. She spit blood and teeth at me as I pressed the tip of my blade up against her abdomen. I watched her expression shift from anger to pain and finally to fear. I drove the blade home, up under her ribs and into her heart. She cursed me out as I watched the life drain from her eyes. Pulling my knife free, I let go of her coat and her lifeless body crumpled to the floor.

I steadied myself on the railing again. It was getting a lot harder to breathe. "**RILEY!**" I yelled after I took a second to catch my breath.

"Shut the fuck up!" I heard from behind me. It was Jimmy, Riley's personal bodyguard. There was a crack and granite went flying. I felt a burning in my right shoulder a second before I heard the report of the gun. I pulled my Sigs from the harness as I turned to face the big man.

He was thirty feet away, at least, and had his gun trained on me. He was walking slowly toward me. Everything started to get blurry and I blinked a few times. He was closer now, and I moved to the side, circling to keep the distance between us. If he got too close, I was all done. I fired off a couple rounds, which started a chain reaction. He returned fire as we circled slowly going back and forth. I watched as one of my rounds hit home making him stumble back a step. I clenched my teeth and forced myself to focus through the pain. He was still yanking on the trigger as I stepped forward and emptied both guns at him. The last round he fired caught me high in the chest and I felt something break. I had landed at least six shots on him. He was slumped on the stairs, his pistol lying next to him on the ground. As I walked up to the large man, a scarlet stain began to pool beneath him on the stone floor. He coughed up blood as he tried to grab at my leg as I got closer. I stared at the man for a good twenty second, watching him bleed out. I leveled my pistol at him and pulled the trigger. He flinched, but there was only a click. I turned the weapon to the side and stared at it blankly. I hadn't noticed that both pistols were locked back, empty. I tossed them both on the ground. I was weaving from side to side and tried to take a deep breath. It ended up being more of a deep sigh.

I lowered myself down onto my knees over him. I could feel the blood soaking into my pants as I straddled him. He tried clawing for his pistol and tried to talk. It came out as more of a gurgling noise that led to a spasm of coughing. "Shhhh," I said softly, pinning him against the stairs. I put one hand on the back of his head and one across his face. I could feel his mouth working beneath it as I tried to take another deep breath. Jimmy continued to struggle slightly, "Shhhh," I said again, same as I would to a small child. Closing my eyes and gathering what little strength I had left, I twisted his head as fast as I could, jerking it almost completely around. There was a loud crack and Jimmy was gone. I stumbled to my feet and roared incoherently.

The yelling led to a fit of coughing that made me want to lie down and die right where I was. I felt, more than heard, someone behind me. I tried to turn, but it was too late. They grabbed me by the hair and yanked my head back hard. I tried to stifle a yelp when I could feel the skin covering my skull starting to tear where the stitches had been. They pulled me back until I was pressed against them. I could feel their breath on the back of my neck, "Do you have any idea, at all, how much trouble you've caused me?" Riley asked quietly in my ear.

When I didn't answer he continued, "Stacey and Jimmy were two of my favorite people. Who's gonna keep the rest of these douchebags in line now?"

He spun me to face the wall and shoved me toward it. I reached back to grab his hand that still felt like it was tearing my skull off. Face first I went into the cold stone wall. Holding me tight against the polished surface, he leaned in close. "Why didn't you just come out when I asked? I would've let the rest of you live if you'd just left the tramp with me... what was her name again? Oh yeah, Eva. All you had to do was let me keep her. You coulda been home safe and sound right now instead of being here bleeding out and dying," he whispered in my ear before punching me hard in the kidney.

"Granted you'd have been going home short 1500 men, or so and with no weapons or gear, cuz no way was I gonna let you keep those, but I'm sure you have more back home in that shit hole you call Boston," he said.

He turned me to face him. He wasn't wearing the sunglasses now, but he still had that big shark like grin that I hated. He laughed and punched me hard in the gut. That set off another round of coughing and he hit me again. Before I knew it, I tried to cough while the air was being forced out of me by Riley's fist, causing me to gag and throw up. Blood spewed out of my mouth, covering Riley's face and chest. He screamed and flailed as he stepped back, quickly wiping at his face. I dropped to my knees and continued to cough and throw up blood. Something was not right inside me, but I didn't think it would matter for too much longer at this point. I could hear him cursing me out as I tried to stay conscious through the dry heaving.

I pushed myself up onto one knee, the fingers in my left hand screaming in protest. I couldn't see them through the glove, but I was pretty sure at least two of them had stopped working. I pulled my knife out of my boot with my right hand. Riley was on me in an instant. Grabbing me by the throat, he pulled me to my feet and pinned me against the wall again. I spun the blade around in my hand and shoved it up toward his ribcage.

I must have been moving slower than I thought, because he swatted my arm away like it was nothing. He roared and punched me in the side of the head, almost knocking me to the floor. I stumbled to the side and caught my feet again enough to stay upright. "You still think you're gonna finish me off you stupid fuck?" he said as he came at me again, "I'm already finished! This was my town! You've fucked everything up you fucking prick!" he said, clubbing me again. "If I could, I'd kill you, bring you back and fucking kill you again for what you've done!" Hitting me again as I tried to stumble out of his way. I heard my knife clang off the polished stone floor. I kept moving, trying to get away from his barrage.

He came over the top of me and drove his fist down into the back of my skull. My left leg buckled and I dropped. My face smashed off the cold stone and it felt like my cheek broke. Riley stopped for a moment, I could hear him chuckle above me a split second before he punted me in the ribs, throwing me into Jimmy's lifeless body, still lying at the bottom of the stairs. I crawled up onto Jimmy, trying to roll over him. Riley's boot smashed into my ribs again. My hands slid out from beneath me and I landed with my face pressed into Jimmy's lap.

I felt his boot on the back of my neck pinning me in place. My hands searched for purchase and I tried to push myself up onto my knees. My right hand brushed against something that wasn't floor, or Jimmy's body. Riley was screaming about something above me as my fingers found it again and moved across it to identify it. I smiled to myself and grabbed a hold. Riley's boot pulled back, to smash my skull and finish me off. I rolled to my right as soon as the pressure was off the back of my neck.

Riley's expression went instantly from rage to fear as soon as he saw that I was holding Jimmy's gun. By then, it was already too late for him. I watched his knee explode with the first shot and he dropped down to my level. The second shot I fired caught him in the gut. He doubled over, howling. I pulled the trigger, trying for a head shot, but the slide had locked back. Dropping the gun, I sighed. I rested my head on Jimmy's thigh for a long moment, before pushing myself up onto my knees.

Everything sounded like it was coming through a string of tin cans. I could hear the pounding of my own heart, as it labored to keep pumping blood out of my wounds and Riley behind me screaming about whatever. It sounded like gibberish as I labored to get myself to my feet one last time. I bent to pick up my knife and nearly fell on my face. Riley grabbed at my pant leg, trying to pull me down as well. Quickly turning, I stabbed him in the forearm and he squealed as he let go.

He had pushed himself back into a sitting position. He was rocking back and forth as he held his exploded knee. "You're fuckin' dead you fuck! I'm so gonna kill you slow for this!" he prattled on as I made my way behind him. He saw me trying to get behind him and scooted along the stone floor, like a dog dragging his ass across a carpet. I dropped again to my knees and grabbed him by the collar with my busted left hand. I pulled him back toward, which me sent pain shooting up my arm. I saw stars and thought that I was going to pass out for a moment.

"No, nononono, let go of me!" Riley said, starting to panic and flail.

I tried to take a deep breath and sighed weakly as I leaned back pulling him almost on top of me, keeping him off balance so he couldn't get away. His bald head rested on my shoulder and he began to blubber. I locked my arm up under his chin and dug my fingers into the side of his skull holding him still. "You," I said softly. All I could taste was copper in my mouth.

"You stabbed me in the back and killed my men," I whispered as I drove my blade deep into the area of his kidney. He bucked and squealed as I turned the blade slowly.

His body went flat again as I pulled the blade free and his breath came out more as a rasp. "You killed my friends," I said as I drove my blade straight down into his abdomen and pulled it up toward me, slicing his intestines along the way. There was no screaming this time. He made more of a gurgling noise as blood drooled out of from between his lips.

I waited for his body to stop spasming from the massive wound before I continued. "Stay with me Riley, just for a little longer," I whispered. "You killed my wife, my family and everyone I hold dear," I paused to choke back tears at the thought of Chris and Lily. "I spent five years protecting them from everything this shithole of a planet could throw at us and you took it all away in a matter of days. I'm not a religious man, but if there was ever anyone I wanted to see rot in hell, it'd be you," I said softly as I dragged my blade slowly across his neck. I held him tight against my chest as he slapped at my arms and clawed at the skin of my forearm, trying to make me let him go. His legs thrummed on loudly against the polished floor. I could hear him choking on his own blood as I leaned back, eyes closed, desperately working to hold him in place until he finally stopped moving.

Thirty seconds, that seemed an eternity passed, and the man who had taken everything from me was dead. I used the last of my strength to shove him off me. I crawled a short distance away and tried to push myself to my feet. My body refused the simple orders I gave it, and I crumpled to the cold floor. I could hear Chris in my head telling me to get up and I started to cry. Quickly, it turned to a retching sob. The coughing came soon and I was gagging on blood. My face, covered in fresh tears, on my hands and knees, bleeding out in a city I'd hated as long as I could remember.

I got the coughing under control one last time before I stopped trying to get up. The floor was so smooth and cool that I decided it would be a great place to lay for a bit. Nothing seemed to hurt anymore. I had no energy to move and all I wanted was to close my eyes and sleep. I nodded slowly as I lowered my head. "I love you angel," I said as I closed my eyes.

## Chapter 16

Black. Not dark black, black like a void, nothingness all around me. I'm not cold or hot, happy or sad, I feel nothing. I hear music. At first, I think it must be angels singing. I soon figure out it's "*What is and what should never be*" by Led Zeppelin.

There's a flash of a face, and blond hair. "**CHRIS!**" I yell and try to reach to her. She's gone as soon as I see it. I yell anyway, at least I think I do. I can't hear anything except a dull roar. For a moment, I see what looks like light. Everything is so blurry. I try and move my hands, but nothing seems to be working.

Black again, then the light, blurry still. I see movement and what may be people. I call out, or try to. Nothings working, why is nothing working? The movement seems frenzied. The figures are dark and sinister. I start to panic. I can hear something over the dull roar in my ears. It sounds like insane gibberish. Are the figures people, or am I in hell? Are these demons?

I start to wail, please God don't let me be in hell. I try to move, to run, to get away and the gibberish gets louder. One leans close and speaks, but I can't understand it. I try and shove it away, but again, my limbs fail me. The face again for a split second, it has to be her. She's blurry too and I can't hear her soft words, but her tone alone soothes me.

Black again, floating along trying to find even a pinprick of light. Glaring light startles me. Shining right in front of me, blinding me, I panic again. I try and turn from it, try and push it away from me. Again, the soothing tone returns. The light is too bright and I can't see her, but it has to be Chris, she's here somewhere. I have to find her! I grope stupidly trying to move my numb body to get to her. I miss her so much already, I have to find her.

The light, she must be there, I try and move toward it. Nothing happens; no matter how I try, I can't seem to get closer. I try harder and push myself, still nothing. I hear the gibberish again, over the roar, as well as something else. A bell, I hear a bell off in the distance. Maybe it's in the light, I can't tell. The gibberish covers it too much. The figure again, blurred and dark. It leans close and I think I can feel its hot breath on my face as it speaks. I try and ask it where Chris is and it makes a hissing noise at me. Panic again, I try to shove it away from me, but my arms won't move, then blackness.

A smell, a sweet soapy smell, I smell Chris. The way she always smells at work. Voices, I hear actual voices, not the insane gibberish of the demons. I can't understand them yet, but they're there. I feel something touch my head and hear one of the voices closer than the rest. I try and speak, I think I'm speaking, but I can't hear my own voice over the others, then darkness again, no dreams, no voices… nothing.

My nose itches, I raise my hand to scratch it, but nothing happens. Wait, my nose itches! I try again to move with no success. I yelled for help and I heard a groan instead, a groan? I try again and the groan gets louder. I still see only darkness. I struggle to try and open my eyes. Light, suddenly real light. Everything is blurry as all hell, but I can start to make out shapes. I yell again and again, but all I hear is the groan. I can tell now that it's at least coming out of me this time.

Voices again, I can almost figure out what they're saying and I yell again. Again, I still only hear myself moaning. The voices sound excited and I hear one of them yell. I see blurred figures come close and suddenly there's a bright light in my eyes. The figure moves the small bright light and I see her, she's fuzzy, but I see her outline. She's short with light colored hair and scrubs, blue scrubs. It has to be Chris, I try and reach out to her and see the lines coming out of my arms for the first time.

She sees me trying to move and talk. I feel her hand on my head and hear her shushing me. I start to cry, she's here with me and I couldn't be happier. My vision is still blurred, but I can hear her more clearly now. She leans in close, her hand stroking my hair. "It's Okay Mr. Mackenzie, you're going ta be okay," she says softly.

"Mr. Mackenzie?" I think to myself. My eyes go wide and I force my hands to my face to rub my eyes clear. It feels like a pound of goo sealing each one shut. I scratched my nose and try to speak again. I quickly realize I can't. I grope for my mouth. That's when I noticed the intubation tube. Small hands grab me by my wrist as I hear her plead for me to calm down. It takes a bit, but I finally do. My vision clears and I see Charlotte sitting on the edge of my bed. Tears flow instantly. I had wanted it to be Chris so much that I had convinced myself that it was real. Seeing Charlotte drove home the reality that my wife was still dead. Once I calmed a bit, I looked around for the first time. The room was small, a bed, IV stand, some equipment and a chair in the corner.

"We had to intubate you, it seems like you should be able to breathe on your own now. If you can just stay calm for a few minutes we can get that out for you. Just nod if that's okay," she said as I nodded.

She left me alone in the room. By the time she came back I was fully awake and really confused. I leaned back and tried to relax as they removed the tube from my throat. I tried to ignore what they were doing to me by singing "*Come together*", the Aerosmith version, in my head. It was a completely unpleasant experience, but they were done quickly, with more discomfort than actual pain.

I tried to speak, but all that came out was a horrid croak. "It's okay, give it a little bit. Don't push so hard," she said with a soft smile, as she put a hand on my forearm. I closed my eyes and swallowed hard, trying to clear my throat.

"What the hell happened?" I managed to whisper.

"From what I saw, death came knockin' for you and you kicked its ass," Charlotte said. "Rest a little longer. I'll tell Sampson you're awake. I'm sure he wants to talk to you." She smiled and left the room.

Everything was fuzzy as I looked around. My left arm and hand were in a cast as well as my leg. I felt my head and it had been shaved. I had been out long enough for a small amount of stubble to have grown back. "Well, look at you!" I heard from the doorway. Sampson came around to the side of the bed all smiles.

"Hey," I whispered.

He handed me a small glass of water and sat on the edge of the bed. "The water will help a bit, sip it though, last thing you want is to throw it up," he said.

I nodded and sipped at the cool liquid. "How about you just work on that for a few and I'll try and catch you up a bit," he said.

"Yeah," I said, before taking another sip.

He snapped his fingers, "I'll have to send out a runner as soon as we're done here, to tell them your okay," he said with a smile.

"A runner, where?" I asked, almost choking on my water.

"To Boston, I'm sure they're gonna want to know you're okay," he said. "We haven't told them we found you yet, because I didn't wanna get their hopes up, in case you didn't pull through."

I was shaking my head emphatically and he looked at me curiously. "No, not yet," was all I could manage. For some reason I was terrified of the people left at home finding out I was alive.

"Umm okay, any particular reason?" he asked.

"I just... I dunno, please just don't okay? Not yet anyway," I said.

"Yeah sure, no problem," he said.

"Thank you. I would like to hear how the hell I got here though," I said, smiling weakly.

"Of course, it's pretty amazing actually. One of Riley's girls found you. Andrea is her name. She came in after everything happened and saw that you had a pulse still. From what she said, she was an EMT before the world went to hell." He paused, letting me absorb the information before he continued. "She stopped your bleeding and got you stable enough, so that her friends there could watch over you, while she went to find a doctor. It took her awhile, but she finally came across someone that knew of a local doctor. Fortunately for you, most of them know who we are," he said, taking his time.

"Andrea? I think I know her," I said softly. My voice was starting to come back and my throat was burning less.

"Yeah, she mentioned that you had met when you first got here," he said, nodding.

"She brought us drinks," I said more to myself.

"Anyway, the doctor got in touch with us to let us know that Riley was dead and we rushed over to see what happened. I swear, I nearly shat myself when I saw you there. I had no idea you had gotten out... I thought you were," he trailed off.

"Dead," I finished for him.

"Yeah," he hung his head and sighed, "I'm so sorry I let you all down."

"Did anyone make it?" I asked, scared to hear the answer.

"One of the buses got through I know that," he said.

"I mean from the wrecks," I said.

"No, not that I know of, again, I'm so sorry Mack," he said, looking devastated.

I had known the answer before I heard it, but it didn't stop the tears from flowing again. Everyone I had ever cared about died on those buses. I tried to speak, but the enormity of it all overwhelmed me and I lost it. Sobbing inconsolably, I leaned into Sampson's shoulder. He wrapped one of his huge arms around me and held me as I dealt with the first of many breakdowns. I felt foolish at first, until I realized, with all the guilt he was carrying, Sampson was crying right along with me.

Once I had calmed a bit, he continued, "It took us a while to clean up and get over to the buses. They had almost burned themselves out by the time we arrived. We stayed until we had everyone we could find out of the wreckage. In total we pulled one hundred and thirty six people out of the two buses."

I nodded silently. "Some we could identify, but most were too badly burned to be recognized. I got the call from the doctors while I was still out there, it was easily around noon by then," he said.

"It took us a few days, but we finally managed to give everyone a decent burial," he said, sounding tired.

"A few days?" I asked. "How long was I out for?"

"You've been out for almost two weeks buddy," he said with a grin.

"JESUS!" I said.

"Yep, two weeks, thought we were gonna lose you more than once, the first couple of days. Charlotte finally got you stabilized, but until then, it was touch and go," he said cheerfully.

"Thank you, I dunno if I should be grateful or angry though. I was kinda ready to go y'know," I said.

"Yeah, that's what I figured too but… it seems that someone else wasn't quite ready to put up with your shit yet," he said, glancing upward.

"Lovely," I said as I rolled my eyes.

"She managed to sew you up pretty well. She took your stitches out a few days ago. We're just waiting for the breaks to heal up. She had to set your hand and fingers, they were pretty fucked up. Your leg and ribs were much less work. Charlotte figures another month in the casts and you should be all healed up," he said.

"She did great work. I won't say I'm happy, but I am truly amazed I'm alive," I said, giving the big man a small smile.

"Oh, you are short one spleen though, that she had to remove. You almost lost a kidney as well, but that came around," he said.

"Wow, good to know," I said.

"Why don't you get some rest, neither you or I am going anywhere anytime soon. I can fill you in on all the details later on. The more you rest the quicker you'll heal up," he said as he stood to leave.

"Yeah, that'd be good. I am kinda tired," I said, nodding.

"I'll be back later," he said, smiling as he walked out.

"HEY!" I yelled after him.

"Yeah?" he asked, ducking his head back in the room.

"How many bodies was it again?" I asked.

"We found one hundred and thirty six. I counted them myself, twice. It was a pretty horrific scene though, there may have been some that just burned up," he answered.

"Thanks" I said.

"Why do you ask?" he questioned.

"Just doin' the math is all," I said, waving him off. "Thanks again."

"No problem, I'll be back a bit later," he said and ducked back out.

I sat quietly for a minute checking my numbers, even with my head being this fuzzy, I was pretty sure they didn't work. It should have been one hundred and forty four, not thirty six. Maybe it was the fuzz in my head. *I'd have to give it more thought when I'm a bit more awake,* I thought to myself as I drifted off to a dreamless sleep.

I slept a lot over the next couple of days, but they still managed to get me out of bed a few times each day, to see if everything was working right. Someone had told Andrea that I was awake and she had come by to see me. She blushed profusely when I thanked her repeatedly for saving my life. They removed the IV's and started me on solid food again as well. I was nowhere near 100%, but I was at least starting to feel human again. Within a week, I was up and about regularly and starting to do light exercise. The two casts made it much more difficult, but it was better than just sitting in bed, rotting away.

I stayed with them for the next three weeks, trying to work my way back to a semblance of healthy. The casts came off and though they ached a bit at first, the bones seemed to have mended. My hair had grown in a bit and I felt much less like a chemo patient. I spent a lot of my time working with Sampson as he toiled away at cleaning up Riley's mess, as well as setting up his own command structure, now that he was in charge of the city. He had served the military well and been a good soldier, but he had no idea how to be a good leader. He was learning and had no trouble asking for my help and advice when he needed it.

About a month after I woke up, I told Charlotte and Sampson that I was leaving. Both were upset, but neither seemed surprised. I had one of Sampson's men take me over to the hospital that Riley had put us up in. It was now just a pile of rubble that blocked off most of the street. Part of our convoy was still parked right where we left it. I smiled to myself when I saw the interceptor was still there as well. I slid into the driver's seat and pulled the visor down, catching the set of keys that fell out smoothly.

Turning the key, the engine roared to life and I nodded in satisfaction. I drove the old Monte Carlo SS back to Sampson's and parked it right out front, with the engine running.

"You sure you wanna leave?" Sampson asked, as I grabbed my duffel bag full of supplies off the bed. "I could use the help around here."

"Nah, you'll be fine. You've got good people here. You did a great job of getting me back on my feet, and now it's time for me to go," I said with a big smile plastered on my face.

"Shouldn't take you long to get home in that beast," he said, hooking a thumb toward the car parked outside.

"Not goin' home," I said, without looking him in the face.

"Funny, I didn't think you were, but I had to be sure," he said solemnly. "This wasn't your fault. You still have people back there that would love to have you home."

"I'm pretty sure everyone that I cared about died down here. I have no reason to go home, and as much as it may not be my fault… It still feels like it is. Like I let those people down and got them killed. Yep, sure feels like my fault," I said as I walked by him.

Charlotte was by the door waiting for me with her pretty yet sad smile. I dropped the bag and lifted her off the ground as I hugged her. "Thanks doc," I said as I kissed her cheek.

"You're very welcome Mack," she said as she returned the kiss. "Where will you go now, if not home?" she asked.

"I dunno," I said with a shrug. "Probably just wander for a bit."

"Well, you have gas and food for a good amount of wandering. I made sure the trunk was filled with full gas cans. I moved your weapons cache to the back seat. Gas and ammo doesn't mix well, in my opinion," Sampson said, shaking my hand.

"Thanks again, both of you," I said as I stepped toward the rumbling car.

"You're always welcome here if you change your mind Mack," he said.

"Good to know sir, I may just take you up on that someday," I said with a soft smile as I shifted the car into drive and pulled away from the building.

I saw them wave to me in the rearview mirror until I turned down another street. I made my way westward out of town. I had no idea where I was going, or what I was going to do. The one fact that was certain in my mind, as much as it pained me, was that I was not heading north east. I was not going home. The thought of it alone, nearly made me nauseous. I could never face those people again, or the ghosts that I knew were there waiting for me. They traveled with me now, gnawing at my subconscious, but they would drive me mad if I were home.

The End 12/16/2012

After the Storm Book 3 "New York" by Don Chase

Made in the USA
San Bernardino, CA
02 May 2013